By PAUL H. ROBESON

We Were Wise Fools
If I Knew Then
The Trip Back

Coming soon -
Watch for:
Shore Enough
Levels of Awareness

The Trip Back

Paul H. Robeson

The Trip Back
All Rights Reserved.
Copyright © 2012-2016 Paul H. Robeson

ISBN - 13: 978-0-9835601-5-9

The text in the book is composed in 12/14.2.
Font type - *Calluna* -Regular, Italic, and Bold
Dutch Designer **Jos Buivenga**, with his serifed text family, **Calluna,** is the by-product of the design process of his **Museo** typeface. While trying different serif shapes he designed slab-serifs with a direction. It has clarity, and makes for comfortable reading. It is also the display font for this book.

PUBLISHED IN THE UNITED STATES OF AMERICA
by Penn Yan Press
Printed in
Charleston, South Carolina

Available from *Amazon.com, PennYanPress.net,* and other book stores

DEDICATION

To my family and mostly to Carol. Carol never lost faith in me even when I lost it in myself.

CONTENTS

Acknowledgements

Barry Clark, Robbinsville, NC
William David and **Deb Barry,** Portland, ME
Christina Haas, East Stroudsburg, PA
Horst Christian and Jenny Link, Cottonwood, CA
Clay Robeson, San Francisco, CA
Richard Kornfield, Waikoloa. HI
Photograph of Paul H. Robeson is by **Kathleen Pair,**
City of Shasta Lake, CA

I THE BROOCH AND BOWL

"Are you there?"

She picked up the brooch and her knuckles started to turn white as she gripped it. Color returned to her hands as her muscles started to relax. She sat in silence, waiting. A warm wind moved the lace curtain and made her brow feel comfortable.

"That was how it always started, Karley."

The young pre-teen sat in silence listening to her mother.

"When I wanted to talk to Kristin I would get the brooch and hold it."

"Did anyone else ever hear her," Karley asked.

"No. I tried once, but I think she became angry."

Kate stared at her daughter but her mind was on that one time in the distant past when a similar meeting was tried.

"Are you there?" She picked up the brooch and her knuckles turned white as she gripped it. Color started to return to her hands as her hand muscles started to relax. She sat in silence, -- waiting. A warm wind moved the lace curtain and made her sweaty brow feel comfortable. The candle in the wall sconce flickered. She turned to the breeze and whispered again.

"Are you there?"

There was no answer, only the sound of some papers blowing off the phone stand. She whirled around at the sound.

"Kristin? Kristin, is that you?"

Now she could hear the distant drums getting louder. She put her hand to her chest, knowing that it was her heart making the noise. She knew the signs, the candle flickering and then -- that sound. It was always there whenever she talked to Kristin. Was Kristin near? The breeze coming in the window was now cold -- another good sign.

"Kristin, I, I *have* to talk to you. Say something, *anything*. Do something, please. I *need* to talk to you."

Suddenly, the breeze turned into a gale-type wind, causing the old window to shutter, shake, and then slam shut. The candle flame flickered, but then recovered its grip on the wick. Kate's hands were up to her face covering it. She sobbed quietly.

"She's angry. She's upset that you are here," she said as she took her hands down and folded them in her lap. She looked up as Richard came out of the dark shadows and crossed the room. He quietly put his hand on her shoulder.

"You may be right, that was the strangest thing I've ever seen," he said to her.

"Okay, I'm sorry. But if she talks to you, then she will understand -- when you tell her what happened. Won't she?"

"*If*, she comes back."

Richard didn't know how to answer. He walked into Kate's kitchen and turned on the light. He poured some coffee into a cup.

"Want some?" he asked.

"No, no thank you."

Richard looked at Kate sitting by the old dining room table as he went over and put the cup into the microwave. He punched a few buttons and the cup started to whirl around on a plate inside the oven.

"She'll come back, I know it. When she knows the reason, she'll be back to talk to you," he said trying to reassure her.

Kate moved her head up and down a few times, placed her elbow on the table and rested her chin in her hand. Richard took the cup out of the microwave and returned to the dining room. He picked up a magazine and quickly placed the cup on it on the table. He pulled a chair from the table and sat down.

"Com'on, she'll be back and she'll help you. I really believe that."

"Please Richard, don't patronize me."

"I'm not. I really think she will come back. Up until tonight -- I was a little skeptical. But when a breeze comes up on a still night and blows the window shut and then the breeze is gone, -- I mean, that was quite impressive."

"You mean you really didn't believe me all this time?"

"No, no, I said I had a 'few doubts.' But they are all gone. I guess it was too much to ask of her to talk to me. I, I never met her ...remember?"

"Yeah, I suppose it *was* too much. I guess I expected her to trust you like I do. I'm sorry."

"Hey, forget it. The important thing is that we get busy and stop this whole mess."

"Do you really think there is a chance or are we just spinning our wheels?"

"No, there definitely *is* a chance. I just have to get busy and stop them."

Kate struggled to her feet. Richard set his coffee down and helped her up.

"Do you need help to your room," he asked.

"No thank you. I had better get more and more independent in case this doesn't work."

"Hey, no talk like that. Everything will be okay."

"Please don't use that expression, that's what the other doctors told me also."

"Again, I'm sorry Kate. I keep stepping on you toes... so to speak." Kate smiled. "Okay! The first smile I've seen tonight. It looks nice on you."

"That is kind of funny too. I've almost forgotten how to smile." Richard picked up the brooch off the table and handed it to Kate.

"Don't you want to put this away?"

"Yes, yes I do, thanks."

"I'll let myself out. Are you sure you will be okay?"

"Com'on Doc, I'm a grown up girl."

"Yeah, and a stubborn one at that." He stopped and thought about what he just said.

"But then again, you wouldn't be where you are today if you weren't stubborn."

Kate smiled as Richard laughed and opened the back door. He checked the door latch to make sure it would lock when he closed it.

"Okay lady, I'll talk to you tomorrow. Now please don't run yourself down."

Richard closed the door and watched through the door window as Kate shuffled across the kitchen and reached for the wall switch. She went into the hall.

Kate didn't turn the light on in her room; she just pulled her right leg behind her as she headed for her dresser. She placed the brooch on a hook beside the mirror and then turned and moved to her bed. As she flopped down on the bed she heard Richard's car drive down the driveway. The sound of gravel being crunched together under the tires was a familiar sound to her. The moonlight gave her room some definition as her eyes become more accustomed to the darkness.

She looked around the room and her eyes were drawn to moonlight reflecting off the silver brooch she had just hung up. A tear rolled down her cheek as she knew her mind was going to go over, for the millionth time, "that day."

"I'll be glad to get back to school," Kristin said as she adjusted the cinch on the saddle, "...I mean, I'll miss our trail rides, but I'm looking forward to this next year."

"Yeah, I know what you mean. But see, if you had decided to go to State, you could do your horseback riding too," Kate said as she mounted her horse. "...but no, you had to go to the big city to school."

"You know State doesn't offer Russian as a language," Kristin said as she mounted up.

"Yeah, but that also means you're going to have to work in a big city when you graduate. They sure don't speak Russian around here."

Almost by rote, the horses headed out the gate and onto a well-used riding path. Green trees in the distance concealed the river from this side of the pasture, but the horses seemed to know it is there and headed for it.

"And you're just as bad Kate. Where are you going to dig up artifacts, ...along the Saco River? No, you'll probably head over to some arid desert in Chad or the Sudan." The sisters laughed as they crossed the field.

"Where to today? Up the river, down the river, or toward Bentonville?"

"It doesn't matter much, why don't we go down river toward Willow Springs?"

"That sounds good. We can cut across the river at Bika Crossing and check out that old cemetery?"

"Maybe you *are* going to dig up relics along the Saco River," Kristen said jokingly.

"Maybe so. They do say that there used to be an old Indian Village at the bend."

"There probably was, I mean who built the old covered bridge anyway? It should have fallen down years ago," Kristin said.

"Well, Indians didn't build it. The early settlers did. It's been condemned since we were kids. The only souls who still use it are the Norton boys when they round up strays that have crossed the river – and us."

"It's a good thing they put that barrier across it to stop cars, their weight alone could send it into the river."

"Uncle Bill said that a group of preservationists are trying to get money to restore it and make it a historic landmark or something. He says the bridge will out last us all," Kate said as she patted her horse.

"I guess it would be nice if they fixed it ...but then we probably wouldn't be able to cross it any more."

"So what, we aren't supposed to cross it now and we do."

They looked down the road at the bridge.

"The covered bridge was once an indication of a community's growth in a civilized world. Now it just sits here old and forlorn."

The two horses walked along as the girls looked at the bridge in silence. Suddenly, Kristin said, "Hey, look!"

Kristin was out of the saddle and down on the ground picking something up. It looked like an old brooch. She pulled out her shirt tail and burnished the object.

"What is it," Kate asked.

"A brooch! It looks like it even could be silver. It isn't rusted ..but it *IS* old."

Kristin spit a little on the brooch and rubbed it harder with her shirt tail.

"It IS silver! Look at it glisten! I can't wait to get it home and clean it up."

"It's beautiful, I'll bet it will look fabulous when it's all polished," Kate said.

"I know it will." Let's cut over to Henryville and stop at the general store and get a bottle of silver polish."

"Okay, let's go," Kate said as Kristin swung her leg over the saddle and was back up on her horse.

The sisters listened to the familiar sound of their horses' hooves on the plank flooring as they started across the bridge.
The sound from the horse's feet seemed to get louder and louder as if the sound was going to rupture their ear drums. They looked at each other as if to ask if the other was hearing it also.

Suddenly, Kristin and her horse were up above Kate and Kate was looking up at them. Then, Kate was above them and looking down. Then they were next to her and she could see Kristin's eyes. Kristin's eyes were huge and her mouth was open but Kate couldn't hear her screaming. Kristin had to be screaming, her mouth was open. No, it was Kate that was screaming but Kate couldn't hear herself; all she heard was the sound of wood breaking and tearing apart. Kate was hearing the sound of the old bridge screaming -- screaming in a death cry.

Everything was turning and turning and she saw Kristin's horse go by and the horse looked like it was screaming also. She saw the water of the river above her. It couldn't be! One has to be above the water to see it. The tearing wood sounds were mixing together with horses whinnying and screams and water splashing. They kept repeating and repeating over and over and they kept getting louder and louder.

Suddenly, she did hear *herself* scream.

She sat bolt upright in bed. She saw the brooch glistening from the moonlight. It was still hanging on the hook on the wall. Kate was completely wet from perspiration and she was cold.

"Why," she thought, "...why do I re-live that day so often? Why couldn't the image of that day die ...like Kristin did? Is that why Kristin always talks to me," she asked herself.

Kate pulled herself out of bed and took off her wet clothes. A warm shower made her stop shaking, yet she knew that this whole scene would be played over again and again, like it had in the past.

The morning sun sent rays of pink and purple light through the hills and bouncing off slow moving clouds.

Kate rubbed the sleep from her eyes. She rolled slowly toward the side of the bed. Her good leg was now on the floor and the morning ritual of getting out of bed continued for what seemed like the 50 millionth time.

In the kitchen, she turned on the coffee maker after she put coffee and water into it. Sitting at the kitchen table, she turned the radio on while she watched the fresh brewed liquid run in a continuous drip into the glass coffee pot.

The morning news continued with more new trouble in the Middle East and then about a storm front moving along the Atlantic coast. After a commercial for a laxative, the local news was next. Kate poured herself a cup of coffee as she listened.

"...and the battle with the State Department of Education and Kate Coletrayn continues. The State contends that the Coletrayn property is the only possible place that Benton Township can place the proposed new College Research Facility. Ms Coletrayn differs. She insists that her property is not for sale, and that there are numerous multi-acre parcels available in the township. State Officials hinted to this reporter that the process of 'eminent domain' is being looked into. Kate Coletrayn, as you may remember, was with her twin sister Kristin when Kristin was killed in the collapse of the old covered bridge at Bika Crossing some twelve years ago. Kate Coletrayn was unavailable for comment about the property."

"Bull crap! Not available. The phone still works. Not one question to me from the media and they make it sound like *I'm* not talking and *I'm* the bad guy in this whole thing. And why did he have to bring up Kristin's death? He made it sound like that was my fault too. Damn!"

She took a sip of coffee as the phone gave the familiar ringing sound. Kate reached up on the wall and took the phone off the cradle.

"Hello."

"Morning Kate," the voice of Richard was heard in the phone. "... did you have a good night's sleep?"

"Good morning. No, not really Richard. I guess I was all keyed up about trying to talk to Kristin. And then I had that 'dream' again."

"I'm sorry. They say the memory of that day will eventually go away ...it's just a matter of time."

"Yeah," Kate replied, "...you sound like an old song -- What's up Doc?"

"I sound like an old song? What's up Doc? Com'on kiddo."

"Sorry Richard. What is happening?"

"Were you listening to the local news on the radio?"

"Yeah, more crap. And they keep bringing up Kristin.

They never called me about the property," she said in disgust.

"I didn't think they had. You would have said something to me last night if they had called."

"I don't know Richard, I feel like the Philistines up against Goliath."

"Well, maybe you can be Sampson. You told me about the day the bridge went down and about the brooch and you told me something else. You mentioned that there was, or could have been, an old Indian Village on the river. Didn't you tell me that?"

"Yes, I did. I was taking a Native American Folk-lore class at State at the time and the professor, Dr. Morgan, talked about doing more research in the area. He thought that a tribe of Pequawkett Indians lived there ...before being driven out by early settlers. Ahh ...why?"

"How come you never did any investigating around there?"

"I don't know, I guess that after Kristin found that brooch, I kind of felt, I don't know, *funny,* about going to the river or even looking around down there."

"Well, it may be a long shot, but if we could find evidence that there was a village, it might help stop the research facility from going in."

"Yeah, but don't you think they would have checked it out ...the first thing ...before deciding on the site?"

"Not necessarily," Richard continued, "...I'm having Bud Zackery look into it. I already called him this morning, and he will be in the Capitol tomorrow and will look into it for us."

"Us? You sound as if this is your battle too."

"Well, in a way it is. You are still my patient, aren't you?"

"Yes, but, I mean you've done so much already, I don't know how I can ever repay you."

"Well, you could start by going to a movie with me on Saturday night," Richard said in a matter-of-fact voice.

"I, ahh, I ...I guess so," came the timid reply.

"You don't have to sound so enthusiastic," Richard said with a disappointed tone in his voice.

"No, I'm sorry it sounded that way, I just feel self-conscious with my leg and all. And I don't want anyone to feel sorry for me."

"Who feels sorry for you? Hey, not to worry about that -- and speaking about that, your leg that is, Jeremy Clark has been looking at your x-rays and feels that there *is* hope that you will lose the limp."

"Oh Richard ...really?"

"Yes, but we'll talk about it Saturday night, -- after the movie, okay?"

"Okay, I'll talk to you on Saturday, and I would love to go to the movies with you Richard."

"That's better. I'll call you tomorrow, about which movie to see, okay?"

I tear rolled down Kate's cheek as she put the phone down and stared out the window toward the distant trees by the river.

She knew there was no sense getting her expectations up. Little 'hopes' like this had happened before and nothing came from it -- she still dragged the leg behind her.

Kate went outside and moved toward the barn.

She had gone to the barn at least twice a day, every day, since she could remember. Well, not every day. There was that year she was in the hospital after the bridge fell, and then several years after she came home -- when she was learning to walk again.

She thought about her mother and father and how happy they were that they still had one daughter and had not 'lost' them both. She remembered how, the first thing they did was to get another horse for her.

Kate thought about wheeling herself out to the corral to watch her father train and work with the new horse. She remembered how she hated that horse, -- how she hated all horses, after what had happened.

The words of her father came back to her as she saw Shasta who recognize her and come prancing over to the gate.

As soon as the saddle was secure she had to have the bridle put on. But Shasta also seemed to know that when they got back she would have a nice brush-down and hay and more oats -- it was a routine that she seemed to enjoy.

Kate climbed up on the mounting stairs that her dad had built for her. She wished that he and mom were still around as she got on top of Shasta. The horse went out the big barn doors and headed for her usual riding trail. This time though, the reigns went across Shasta's neck and she was directed in the opposite direction. Shasta obeyed well.

As Kate rode along the overgrown old road that used to be well-used and worn, she recalled talking with Kristin the last time the two of them rode here. She could feel her heart beat faster as she rode the trail that had changed her and Kristin's lives so dramatically.

Kate thought about the people's face staring down at her and how they went spinning around her head as she went in and out of consciousness. She remembered the distant sound of a gun shot, and an ambulance, and people trying to stick tubes and things in her nose and down her throat. She returned to reality as the horse stumbled over a rock.

"Easy, girl. I know this is all new to you -- and I bet you can tell that I'm tense too, can't you." She patted the horse's neck. "Easy girl, you'll be okay."

In many ways Shasta was a lot more sure-footed than Princess was. She did miss Princess. Kate had had Princess most of her life -- till that day.

Kristin got her horse the same day that Princess arrived. She remembered her parents bought the horses and surprised them with them on their birthday. Prince and Princess. A smile was on her face, but she tasted the tear that rolled down to her lip.

She stopped the horse and looked up to where the old covered bridge once stood at Bika Crossing.

A two lane concrete bridge now spanned the river and she could see an old red pick-up going across it toward Henryville.

She brought the reigns across Shasta's neck and started to turn into the field. She could not go near the bend. Kristin died there and she was crippled there. That place was bad!

She rode across an old run-off culvert in the ditch, and carefully had Shasta step over the old fence that lay rusting in the grass.

She thought to herself, "If I were an Indian, where would I have made my camp?" She recalled that "Bika" was an Indian word for "crooked" or "bend."

She also knew many things had changed since Indians roamed this land.

She thought, "There is that small hill toward the middle of the field, which would have been a likely place for a camp."

Things had grown up so much since her father had farmed here.

As she rode up the slight grade, she remembered how her dad always kept the property so neat and trimmed. Kate thought about how the family always called this part of the farm, the 'potato field.' Her father said that the soil was just right for growing potatoes. She wished she had been more interested in what her mom and dad were doing with the farm, but when she was growing up she did not want to be stuck 'on the farm' all her life. It was kind of ironic, because here she was --'stuck' on the farm and not knowing how to farm it. Maybe she *should* sell the property to the State for their 'research facility.' The only thing she had here were memories. Good memories of her mom and dad and her sister ...and bad memories of her sister's death and then her parent's deaths, five years later.

She was now at the top of the slope and there was "sitting rock" in front of her. It was a large flat boulder about ten-feet wide and around five-feet wide.

Her dad would always have lunch at the rock after Kristin or she would bring it out to him when he was plowing or planting potatoes.

The girls would eat with him and he would always tell them wonderful stories. She remembered her dad telling those stories about the early settlers and the Pequawetts and the Almouchiquois. He always talked about Pequawett and Almouchiquois Indians being around the area. She had not thought about it before, but maybe they did camp here like her dad had said.

Kate guided Shasta up to the rock and then she used the rock to make an easy dismount. She tethered Shasta loosely to a little sapling so the animal could nibble on the tall grasses. Kate sat on the rock and looked around the field. The area was really becoming overgrown. Within a few years it would be a young forest again and not a 'potato field' anymore.

She glanced toward the sky as the sun disappeared behind a slow moving cloud which cast a shadow over the entire area.

"Even you feel sad about it, huh," she said looking toward the cloud.

Shasta turned her head to look at Kate to see who Kate was talking to. She then continued to munch on the grass.

Kate pulled her knees up to her chin, put her arms around her legs and rested her chin on her knees. She sat there for a moment and then she felt a soothing feeling as the sun moved from behind the clouds and sent warmth back to earth. It also radiated a sparkle to her eye. The sun reflected off a green-colored object in the grass about 10 or 12 feet away.

"Darn kids with their beer parties, they don't care where they throw their empties," she thought as she moved her head out of the reflection path, "Pop sure wouldn't have put up with it. I sure do miss him."

Another cloud covered the sun again and she could feel the early autumn coolness from the unheated field. As she started to get to her feet the sun's rays returned and so was the reflection.

This time the reflection was pink.

In a standing position she could see that the reflection was not coming from a bottle but from a different shaped object. It looked almost round. Kate sat back down and lowered her legs down off the rock. She broke a dry sapling and used it as a walking stick as she stumbled toward the object. She bent over and whisked the dry soil off of the thing. It looked like a small, half buried, glass bowl or cup.

"Who would bring a glass bowl out here," she though as she carefully took a small stick and picked away more earth from around and from inside of the vessel.

"We never brought anything that was glass out to dad," she thought, "he was always afraid that we would break something and get cut," she said aloud.

It was glass of some sort she thought, but it wasn't manufactured glass. It was cut or ground into a bowl shape. Soon the container was free from its earth entrapment. She held it up and looked closely at it. It was round on the bottom and there was no place for it to sit without rolling over. Kate scratched the edge with her fingernail and then rubbed it between her index finger and her thumb. Where she rubbed it, it began to shine in the sunlight and she could see a small hole drilled through it near the brim. As she turned it in her hands the reflecting colors changed from greens to browns to pinks. It almost looked like tourmaline.

Kate knew that tourmaline was mined up on the mountain and she had seen fairly large pieces of it, but she had never seen anything this large or cut into a bowl shape.

"It can't be tourmaline, but it must be some sort of crystal," she thought as she looked around the depression in the ground where she had taken it from.

Suddenly, a giant cloud quickly covered the sun making the field look frightening in the shadows. A slight breeze kicked up and sent falling leaves whisking past her. Shasta suddenly started to whinny and prance. Shasta pulled on her reins which broke the sapling that they were tethered to. Shasta bounded up on her hind legs terrifying Kate. Kate had never seen her horse behave this way. The horse bolted across the field as Kate stumbled and fell in a desperate attempt to stop her.

"Shasta," she screamed as the white animal vanished into the woods. Kate was on her hands and knees and all she could think about was, "the gods are REALLY mad at me."

"He'll come back," she heard a voice say. Kate spun around abruptly landing on her behind. There was no one there.

"Kristin," she said, "...Kristin, is that you?"

The wind picked up again and, what seemed like hundreds of leaves went swirling around her. This time the voice seemed to be coming from behind "sitting rock."

"You are near," the voice said and then it started to weaken, repeating, "...you are near."

By now, Kate was on her feet and she stumbled toward the large rock. There was no one behind it. She leaned against the rock and wept quietly as the sun, once again, came out from behind the cloud. With her head down on her arms she again thought about Kristin.

She reeled around at the feeling of warm breath on her neck. Shasta put his head against her almost in an apologetic nudge.

"Shasta, oh Shasta, are you okay," she asked as she hugged the big animal around the neck.

Shasta moved her head up and down as if to tell her everything was okay. Kate tried to get her composure back and she took big gulps of air.

"The bowl!" she said aloud as she looked around for it. She didn't remember dropping it but with the horse running and the gust of wind, she must have -- it was gone. She spotted it about six or seven feet away, down in a little run-off trench.

She stumbled over to it and stooped down to pick it up. As she touched the bowl she got a little buzzing sensation much like a mild electrical shock. The reaction made her hand come away quickly form the object. She noticed a dark hole in the side of the trench.

Her mind asked the question, "Was I bit by something?" A quick inspection of her hand revealed there were no blemishes or puncture marks. She picked up a near-by stick and probed into the black hole. She didn't hit anything, just the sides of the opening. Assuming there was nothing in the hole she tossed the stick into it. There was no sound of it hitting the earth.

"Oh well," she thought, "I do have to have my hearing checked."

She picked up the glass bowl. It was not damaged by the fall, so she got back to her feet and trudged back to where Shasta was patiently waiting. She placed the bowl on Sitting Rock and then pulled herself up onto the rock. Shasta moved alongside to await her mounting. Once on Shasta's back she reached down and picked up the glass bowl.

2 WHERE DOES IT HURT?

He sounded like a talking encyclopedia as he lectured about Indians. It was almost as if he had lived with them a century ago.

"Colonel John Allan told us that the Indians dressed in hand-outs and gifts. They wore blankets, red coats and laced hats but they never wore, as we have been lead to believe, '...buckled shoes and cocked hats.'

"On 'special' occasions they would appear in very opulent and ornate European clothing. Their old 'skins and furs' were being replaced with cloth garments in their everyday life. They had, by the 1830's, discarded their aboriginal garb, except for their moccasins. By that time they never wore dressed skins as garments."

The professor turned to a large map of Maine on the wall behind him and continued.

"The town of Brewer had more Indians living there than white people." He turned back to the group and said, "Men wore long, loose, frock coats that reached their knees and they were made of broadcloth. Their coats had no buttons on them, and were confined by leather belts. An 'exceptional' coat might have had bead work lapels or even a collar. An 'exquisite' coat could be bright red and beaded and banded with ribbons."

A hand went up in the back of the room and a question was asked, followed by a giggle from the corner.

"What did they wear underneath the coats, Dr. Morgan?"

"I was coming to that Miss Anderson," he said. "Under their coats they might, or might not, wear a shirt, a cotton shirt and that was all."

A few faint gasps and a snicker or two were heard. Several hands went up.

"Were the Indians the first known flashers?" someone asked.

"No. Actually in 1540 in England there was a reported case of a man that..." He stopped when the laughter rose in the room.

"Ahemmm," he continued, clearing his throat, "...All the clothes that is. They wore gee-strings about their waists to support leggings or breech cloths. The breech cloth was a wide piece of cotton cloth passed between the legs and up under the gee-string in the front and back."

He looked around the room to see if he had satisfied the questions and if the group was going to get serious again. He had and they were.

"Now, I'm talking about the adult male of this time period. By the 1850 most of these older males were dead, but the younger men had, by then, adopted trousers. Again now, in the 1830's, the leggings were fastened by thongs to the gee-strings. The leggings came down to about their knees. They still wore moccasins, but their feet were wrapped in cloths before stockings, or socks as you young people call them, were adopted.

They didn't wear hats in the summer, but in the winter their heads were protected by close fitting caps with two points ...like ears. The caps had capes in the back to keep the snow out of the back of their necks."

"What did the women wear?" a question was asked.

"Women wore pretty much the same in the summer and the winter. They wore loose sacques, or sacks, that fell half-way to their knees and a short, scant skirt that dropped below the knees. They wore leggings and moccasins and also blankets and caps in cold weather. Most of their clothing might be something that the white people had discarded. The garment might be slightly remodeled, to their way of living, but their 'good' dresses were described as 'sumptuous.' The sacque was made out of red or blue broadcloth and was usually trimmed with beads and ribbons and ornamented with numerous silver brooches."

The words 'silver brooches' abruptly brought Kate back to the classroom from her fantasy trip with the New England Indians. Her hand flew into the air.

"Now these... ahh, yes Miss Coletrayn?"

"Silver brooches, you said silver brooches. What did they look like?"

"I was getting to that. Now, both men and women wore many, and costly, silver ornaments. The men wore arm bands, medals and sometimes brooches. The women also wore bracelets, hat bands, otter tails for their hair and many silver brooches. They had all sizes of them, from two inches to eight inches in diameter. They were circular, convex in the middle, and were pierced and chased. They had round holes in the middle with a pin, like a buckle tongue. They would pull a portion of the cloth up through the hole and thrust the tongue through the cloth, which was then pulled back into place, holding the pin down.

Brooches were worn all over the front of the body, even on their skirts...if they were wealthy enough. This was considered 'Indian high fashion' between 1840 and 1850, but it went out of style about the same time as the start of the Civil War."

The professor's words went on, but they were somewhere in the background, as Kate thought about Kristin's brooch.

"Kate. Kate, I have wanted to give you this for a long time, but I, I wasn't quite sure how to do it. It's been almost two years now and well..," Kate's mother held out her hand and put the silver brooch into Kate's hand. "I'm sure Kristin would have wanted you to have it. I don't know how to say this, but they, they had to pry it out of her hand when ...when they found her."

Kate was speechless for a moment and then a horrible feeling of devastation came over her as she turned the silver brooch over and over in her own hands. She broke into uncontrollable sobs of grief. Her mother tried to console her.

"Easy baby. I, I wouldn't have given you this if I had known that it would bring back such bad memories." Kate continued to cry as she clutched the brooch and held it to her breast.

"I had never seen it before... that day. Where did she get it?" Through her sobs, Kate tried to answer.

"She, she found it by the bridge, just ...just before we started to cross. We, we were headed for the general store to get silver polish to clean it. It's beautiful ...like Kristin said." She turned and cried into her pillow.

"Kate? Kate Coletrayn. Are you okay?" the professor asked. Kate looked, through her tear-filled eyes, and could see that everyone in the room was looking at her. She nodded her head yes, but held it low in embarrassment.

"Class. Class. ...Ahh, that will be all for today. On Monday we will discuss the keeping of tailless eagles in the Micmac camps and the use of their feathers in the making of arrows. Have a good weekend everyone."

The other students picked up their books and belongings in silence and filed out of the room. A few of them turned to look at the professor going between the chairs toward the sobbing young woman in the wheelchair.

"Kate? Are you sure that you are okay?"

"I'm sorry, sir, I didn't mean to disrupt your class."

"No problem, Kate. Is it something that I said?" Kate nodded and he continued. "Does it have to do with brooches?" Kate nodded her head again.

"My sister, my sister Kristin had found a brooch just, just before we, we..."

"Found a brooch, where?" he asked, not being sure of what to say.

"At Bika Crossing," she answered as she tried to regain her composure.

"Bika. 'Bika' is a Pequawkett word for 'crook' or 'bend...' It comes from the word 'bikahlagenigan' or 'biketagenigan,' which was the name of the 'crooked' shape of the handles of their knives. They probably named the bend in the river 'Bika' and it became 'Bika Crossing.' Now, I'm..., I'm sorry."

He stopped, when he realized that he was being a teacher while his student was suffering. He changed the subject.

"Kate, do you think you should, maybe drop this course ...for a while ...until you feel better. It has only been a short time since..."

"I'm fine professor," Kate answered.

"But Kate, we do have the 'dig' coming up and it is in the mountains and..."

"Please don't worry about me, sir, I only use this chariot in school. I use crutches all other times. I can manage it. Besides my Doctor is doing a NEJM paper on me and he wants to accompany me on the trip ...so he can help me also."

"Well, I guess you will do fine then. And ah, do you still have that brooch?"

"Yes. My mother gave it to me. I always thought it was from one of the early settlers, but I didn't know how early."

"Well, Kate, why don't you go on home and have a good weekend. And, if you think about it, maybe you could bring the brooch in sometime ...for me to look at ...okay?"

Kate smiled and wheeled herself toward the door.

Kate had to focus through her tears as she looked up the path toward the house. There was a car in the driveway that she did not recognize. She wiped her eyes and tried to gain control over herself as she neared the vehicle. Two men in dress suits were leaning against the front of their car watching her as she approached them.

"Ms Coletrayne, we represent the firm of *Waterman and Gassaway,* from Baa-ston." they said as she stopped Shasta. Kate sat on the horse and just looked at them.

"Ah, we would like to discuss the possibility of purchasing your property ...but I understand that the *Bureau of Native* New England Americans will not allow the purchase pending the completion of the Environmental Impact Report on the property."

There was still no response.

"Ahhh, we are aware that you do not want to sell, but we are prepared to offer you twice the appraised price of the property."

Kate sat back in the saddle reminiscent of John Wayne or Tom Mix.

"Now," she said, almost in a Texas drawl, "...just who appraised the land, for how much, and who authorized it?"

The two men looked at each other with blank expressions on their faces. They said a few "ahh's" and "ahem's" and then she said, as she reached to the back of the saddle where they could not see her hand, "...I don't mean to be rude gentlemen, but GET THE HELL OFF OF MY PROPERTY!"

The two men quickly got into their car, never taking their eyes off of the hand they couldn't see. Kate had to duck as a few pebbles were thrown up by their car tires as the car sped down the gravel driveway. She continued her ride into the barn and stopped at the mounting stairs. She slowly dismounted and walked down the steps.

"Pretty impressive, Pilgrim." Richard said as he sucked on a piece of a hay stem. He was laying on a bale of hay and had seen the whole scene through the open barn doors.

"Richard! What are you doing here?"

"I just watched the 'cool lady' blow the poachers' right out of the valley." he said as he got up from his prone position.

"They have been waiting for you for about an hour. They got here just after I did. I told them you would not be interested, but they insisted on waiting anyway. I figured I had better stick around and keep an eye on them."

"Gad, I hope you are 'off the clock,' I would go broke with your bill. Richard laughed as Kate hung up her saddle bags. She was about to say something to Richard when he jumped back and held his shirt button.

"Listen, sweet-ha-at," he said in a poor Bogart imitation, "even my own mother can't afford my prices ...because I'm the best their is ...see?"

Kate went over to Richard, as he finished his 'hamming,'and gave him a big hug. He held her and he gently patted her on the back.

"I don't know what I would do without you," she said as Richard gave her another squeeze.

"Well, if someone from the *AMA* saw me now they might say that I was abusing the 'Doctor - Patient' relationship."

Kate laughed as Richard helped her put the saddle up on a rack. She tossed the saddle blanket over the saddle and then, methodically went for grain and a flake of hay for Shasta. She reached for a curry comb as Richard said, "Been out all morning?"

"Just about. I rode over to Bika Crossing. You know, this is the first time I've seen the new bridge."

Richard watched her as she combed Shasta.

"Oh, I almost forgot. Look what I found." Over at the saddle bag rack, she opened one side of the bag. Richard's eyes widened as she pulled out the glass bowl.

"Wow! Where did you find that," he asked as she handed it to him.

"In the potato field, on the hill."

Richard has a questioning look on his face as he said, "The potato field?"

"Oh, I'm sorry. We used to call the lower field, the one closest to the river bend, the 'potato field,' Dad always grew potatoes there."

"It looks like crystal or, by the colors, it could be tourmaline," Richard said looking at the object.

"That's what I thought at first. But, I am no stone or gem expert."

"You do know Indians, though. Could it have been made by Indians?"

"I don't know, I don't recall any literature being written about the Pequawketts or Almouchiquois using glass like this. I mean, if it was a woven porcupine quill box, a priming flask or a powder horn, I might be able to identify it. This could even be one of those new acrylic plastics -- like you used on my head."

Richard gave a forced laugh and then came back with, "Your head is so hard, I don't know how it could have shattered."

"Touché. But it could be of a totally different origin than Indian. We may be just thinking that it is Indian because we WANT it to be Indian," she said.

"You're right. But I do know that the Pequawketts traded with the French for copper bowls and even glass ones. But I think this one is too primitive to have come from Europe."

"Yes, it could have come from Mattel or it could even be from Tonka," Kate quipped.

"Okay, okay smart as..."

He stopped what he was going to say.

"Is there anyone that can look at it and possibly identify it?"

Kate thought before answering.

"I don't know if Dr. Morgan is still at State or not, but I could give him a call."

"Yeah, he was real helpful on that dig a few years back."

"No more than you were to him. If you hadn't been there he probably would have bled to death after his fall. I'm sure he would return the favor."

"Well, I figured I would do 'anything' to get you through that course," he said trying to keep from smiling.

"Thanks a lot. I was doing just fine before the dig and I would have made it even without you," she shot back.

"Hey, get your feathers down. I was just kidding. Do you think I would really say something like that if I felt you were actually in trouble with your class work?"

"I'm sorry. It's just that that was a very hard time for me. It was just after mom had given me the brooch they took from Kristin's hand."

"I know. And it was the first time I ever went 'out' with you, socially."

"Socially. You call trekking up on top of *Black Peak* to look for Indian artifacts, social? Com'on Richard, we were both working. You were doing that paper for the *New England Journal of Medicine*, and I was working on my masters' degree."

"You know what I mean. Until that time you were just a patient that I wanted to study and, well, Dr. Morgan's accident changed quite a few things."

"Oh?" she said, not knowing for sure what he meant.

"I, I saw you in a different light," Richard continued, "Half of the kids on that dig started to panic. And you, you with your gimpy leg, were the one that climbed down on that ledge to hold on to him until we could get down there to give him medical attention. That's when I realized I had an even better paper in the works ...how to find out what kept you going. You became very interesting to me."

"That's what it is, huh? I'm your next research paper so you can get that job as Department Head."

"Ouuuu that hurt. We have been ...friends now for almost seven years, do you really think that?"

"Gottcha didn't I." Kate said as she ducked under a stall rail, giggling.

"You little twerp," Richard said as he grabbed for her and missed. "Yes, you did get me. I thought you were serious when you said that."

"I was, but not how you think. If I could do anything to get you to the job you wanted I would do it. I do 'owe' you."

"Hey, you don't owe me anything, Kate."

"Good, now I can turn the tape recorder off... and write your bills off."

"You clown. Got me again. ...I don't know." He had Kate by the shoulders and pulled her to him.

They kiss - like friends.

"Where does it hurt?" he asked as he bent over her. She looked up at his big, blue eyes. He had tubes coming from his ears.

"In my mind," she answered. The young doctor stood up and smiled and gave a little laugh.

"Ha ha. You sound like Bertrand Russell."

"Who," she asked, "...the English philosopher?"

"Yes. Well, I see you are not just another pretty face."

"Pretty?" She picked up a hand mirror from the bed-stand.

"You know what I mean. You'll have your looks back as soon as all the swelling goes down."

Kate started to cry as she looked at the bandages that covered her head. Her eyes had black and blue skin all around them.

"Easy now," Richard said as he took the mirror from her hands. "At least you knew who Bertrand Russell was, that shows me that your mind is working. I would say that 95 percent of my patients don't even know Russell."

"Ninety-five percent?" Kate said quickly, "How many patients do you have? Three?"

"Owww, low blow."

"I'm sorry Doctor. I'm just really depressed."

"I know that Kate, and it is natural. After someone has their skull rebuilt with plastic there has to be depression. No pun intended...Ahh, not depression as in a dent, but you will experience some, ah ...frustration. ...Ahh, discouragement. You are going to be disappointed with me, with doctors in general, with hospitals and most of all with yourself. ...I mean I..."

He stopped talking and grinned at Kate. "I don't know Kate; you are the only patient that can rattle me. I just can't figure you out. Just when I think I know what you will say, you come out with the complete opposite thing that I was thinking."

"You are the one that told me that the verbal half of my brain, my left half, was not injured. Are you now trying to tell me that it was? I could have told you that and saved myself some money to boot."

"No, no no! You weren't brain damaged at all. I told you that you weren't. ...See what I mean? You were the one that knew about 'split-brain' and I was just trying to explain to you that communication between the two hemispheres 'melds' two perceptions together make us a 'one being' person...a unified entity."

"Yes, but you also said that the left brain was verbal and analytic while the right brain is nonverbal and global. The right side of my skull was shattered and I can talk and you say I can 'think,' what ever that means, and yet I can't walk and there is no physical injury that you guys can find. So, it has to be in my mind... doesn't it?"

"Yes, NO!" Richard was now pacing around the hospital bed. "No, it doesn't. I swear, they never covered anything like your reasoning and rationale in med school. I sure hope that you continue with college when you get back on your feet. I mean..."

Kate smiles. "Oh?" she said.

"You know what I mean. Your brain alone will get you walking again." His voice became louder. "I, I think you are just feeling sorry for yourself." As Richard was bellowing at Kate, Dr. Feldman, Chief-of-Staff, heard him and entered the room.

"Doctor. That will be enough. I would like to see you in my office... NOW!" Richard turned quickly and walked out of the room. Kate realized that she provoked the young doctor and wanted to call out to him. After all, he was the only one she could intellectual conversation with and she just gotten him into trouble.

"Are you okay," Dr. Feldman asked as he picked up her chart to find out her name, "...Kate."

"Yes, I'm fine thanks to Doctor Sprague. We were just discussing Emil Kraepelin's theory of manic depression or 'hypomania.' I told him that *Johns Hopkins University* Professor Kay Redfield Jamison's views differed from Kraepelin's, and that she felt that 'bipolar illness' was of major importance. We just had a difference of opinion. I know Doctor Sprague is much more knowledgeable than I am ...and he is probably right. Ahh.. When you see Dr. Sprague will you tell him that I would like to continue our discussion at a later date. Now, Dr. what can I do for you?"

The confused Chief-of-Staff quickly walked back and forth and then headed for the room door.

"Ahh yes, I will tell him. And, ah, nothing. I just wanted to see how you were doing.

Dr. Sprague said that you had one 'beautiful brain' and I, I believe him. I, I'll tell him you'll continue your discussion ...later. Bye, ahh, Kate." The Doctor quickly exited.

Kate stared at the little holes in the ceiling tiles and wondered if Dr. Sprague would get into trouble or if she 'pulled the wool' over Dr. Feldman's eyes. She smiled.

Picking up her cup of coffee she asked Richard: "Do you remember when old Feldman came into my room when you were yelling at me?"

"Remember," Richard responded with, "...you almost got me fired. It was lucky for both of us that you had told him about Kraepelin's research. I only wish I had known about it, I told him we were discussing Dr. Spector's 'neurolymphomatosis.' I think, between the two of us, we had the poor old guy so confused he didn't know if he should can me or make me head of the department."

Kate laughed and took another sip of coffee.

"What brought that up?" Richard asked.

"Oh, I was just thinking how really depressed I was after the reconstructive surgery."

"I'll say. I couldn't believe your mood swings. You were so happy to be alive one minute and in the next instant you were plunging into a bottomless crater. I thought for a while there that you even had suicidal tendencies."

"Is that why you had the nurses' remove the scissors and my nail file and everything?"

Richard was embarrassed.

"I, ...well, I, ah, I didn't want you to hurt yourself."

"I'll bet. You were on your 'way up' and you didn't want my death on your record."

"Owww, that was cheap. You know that I was interested in your well being." Kate continued to string Richard along.
"My 'well being.' All you wanted me for was so you could do that *New England Journal of Medicine* thesis and make a name for yourself." Richard had a hurt look on his face and didn't try to conceal it.

"Kate, I never tried to use you ...I, I..."

Kate saw the wound that she has inflicted. She was out of her chair, and around to the other side of the kitchen table. She came around to the back of Richard and put her arms around his neck.

"I was kidding Richard! I just saw an opening in your armor and I went for it. I'm sorry Richard, I really am." Richard lowered his head and spoke softly. Kate, still holding Richard's neck, moved her head more to the side of his to hear what he was saying.

"You know, ...it is pretty sad that I have to..." His voice dropped in pitch and Kate had to ask him what he said.

"I'm sorry Richard, I can't hear you."

"I said, that it is pretty sad that, after all the years we have known each other, that I, ...I still have to pretend that I am wounded ...to get you to come to me and put your arms around me."

Kate hands came up to Richard's neck in mock choking.

"Owooo. I should have known. You talk about me not knowing what I'm thinking. Here I am thinking that I hurt you and all you wanted was for me to come over to you."

"Is that so bad? I have been trying to get you to show some interest in me for six years, and all I get is some intellectual discussion about the 'Corpus Callosum,' the Anterior Commissure,' or the 'Hippocampus.' I mean, at this rate, I'll be to old to even be a father."

Kate pulled away and turned toward the kitchen sink. Richard was out of his chair and was behind her. He held her by the upper arms. She was quietly whimpering.

"Kate, I'm sorry. But, you keep giving me that crap about not being a 'total' woman because of your head and because of your limp. ...And that is just what it is, 'crap.' Don't you see that I am 'crazy' about you, and not from a medical point of view."

Kate turned in Richard's arms and softly cried on his chest. He held her and the only sound that was heard was her quiet sobs and a cricket, somewhere in the kitchen.

Richard and Kate flinched from the loud sound of the phone. She moved from Richard's grasp to answer it. She wiped her eyes.

"Hello," she timidly said into the receiver.

"Yes, this is Kate." Richard watched her as she talked. She waited, as if there was no one on the other end of the phone.

"Hi Bud! How are you? Yes, Richard said that you were going to Augusta. No, No we are not married." She turned in mock disgust and looked at Richard. "Right, he isn't my type. You're right, I'm looking for someone handsome like you.

"No. He's right here. Do you want to talk to him? Okay, I understand. Sometimes I feel like I don't want to talk to him either." This time the hurt on Richard's face was real. Kate sensed it, but then as not quite sure if it was real or not.

"Just kidding Bud. Okay, down to business. You what?" Kate repeated what Bud Zackery was saying so that Richard could hear. "You went to the Native New England American office and... There possibly could have been some type of encampment along the river near Bika Crossing? Yes, yes, go on. What? From the *Description and Natural History of the Coasts of North America,* Paris, 1672. Paris, Maine or Paris, France? No, it would have to be France. Oh, okay. I remember now. The University has the W.F. Ganong translation from Toronto. Wasn't it written somewhere between 1905 and 1910? Nineteen-oh-eight. Okay. Yes, I'm acquainted with it, it has a lot of porcupine quill box descriptions in it." She smiled at Richard who was sitting on the edge of his chair listening intently to the one-sided conversation. "Really? 'Big Thunder's' relative? Wow. Eighty-seven? Did he understand the question? Really?" She covered the mouth piece and turned to Richard. "He pointed out Bika Crossing, on a map, to Bud. NO, no, I'm here. I just told Richard about the map. They let you copy it? Wonderful! Okay, okay. Yeah, thanks Bud. We'll see you when you get back. Thanks. Thanks a million. No, no I don't have a million. You clown! You're as bad as Richard. Okay, bye." She hung the phone up and leaned against the sink cabinet.

"Well." Richard said in anticipation. "What did he say?"

"He said that there could have been an encampment around Bika Crossing. One of 'Big Thunder's relatives, who's 87, remembers his grandfather talking about the camp there. He even pointed out Bika Crossing to Bud. He said it was a high religious place or something for the tribe. He does not know why they moved from there. He said something about the gods were angry and swallowed one of the men." She stopped and thought about it and continued. Richard listened in silence. "He probably fell into the water during the spring run-off and was carried down the river. Sorry, I was just finding a way to let myself down from more false hope."

"Hey lady, don't give up so easy. Your sister did find a brooch there and it was of Indian origin. And what about that container. We have to get it checked out. I do have to go into Gorham, do you want me to take it to the University?"

"Yeah, I guess you could. If you could take it to the Anthropology Department in *Bailey Hall*, I could call and see if Dr. Morgan is still there and ask him to meet you. When are you going?"

"This afternoon. I'll be coming back late tonight. Remember now, we have a real date tomorrow evening."

"I will. I mean, I know we have a 'real' date. Richard, I uh... Ahh... we *do* have to talk, you know."

"Have to? I've been trying to talk to you for years and all you do is skirt around the issue at hand."   "I told you, I'm not the issue. You and your work are the issue and I would only be in your way. I'm not in the same class as you are."

"Bullcrap!"

"Well, I'm not. I don't have the money, or the social status or even the figure to fill out one of those gowns I see Darlene Peabody wearing."

"That's not true and you know it."

"What ...the money part, the social status part or the figure part?"

"You know what I mean. I have to go to those affairs with Darlene because of the money her family is donating to the hospital."

"Affairs?"

"Owww! You exasperate me sometimes."

"Only sometimes," Kate said with a little smile, "...I thought I did it to you all the time."

"Sometimes I would like to take you over my knee and spank you."

"AhHa! You're into that kind of stuff too, huh?"

"Owwww. Why Kate? Why do you treat me like this?"

"I'm sorry Richard, I really am. It's just that you think there can be more between us and I don't think there can be."

"Don't think? How do you know unless you try. I still say that it is only fear. You are afraid to try loving someone because the only people you ever loved ...died."

Kate was stunned at Richard's remark. He moved over to a kitchen counter where the bowl that she had found was in a box. She turned and looked out the kitchen window.

"Kate, I'm sorry. I *do* have to go, and I will drop this off at the University and, and ...we will be seeing each other tomorrow night, ...won't we?"

She nodded her head, perhaps realizing that what Richard has said may have had some truth to it. Richard was out the door before Kate could thank him for taking the bowl and for all his help in what could be a very lonely battle.

Kate moved into her living room and watched out the front window as Richard's car drove down the driveway. Maybe Richard was right, maybe she was afraid of love.

She knew she loved him, at least as to what she thought love was. She liked to be around him and she liked to talk to him. He was intelligent and kind and fun. He had brought her back from her depths of depression. Maybe she wasn't being fair to him. Kate tried rationale in her thoughts. She liked Richard and she knew Darlene Peabody had an invested interest in him. She disliked Darlene and she figured the reason for the dislike was because of her money ...or her parent's money. They girls had gone through school together and then Darlene went on to *Smith College* while Kristin and she went to state schools. Darlene's picture was always on the social page for work with such-and-such charity or as the 'woman of the year' in business. Kate admitted to herself that she was jealous of Darlene. Perhaps even more so, now that she was showing such a big interest in her 'friend' Richard.

She knew she had an attachment to Richard, but she did not know what love was. Perhaps he was right, she was afraid that she would lose him like she lost Kristin and her parents. She also knew that she could lose him to Darlene. Why did everything have to be so complicated? She wanted to love Richard in the physical sense, but she knew that she had real fears on that subject. She was not 'complete' in her own mind. She had scars on her body and her leg didn't function right and her worse fear was that she was brain damaged from the accident. Everyone told her that she wasn't. But when something like that happens to someone, everyone feels sorry for them and tries to help. She remembered how, after the accident she would 'double check' everything. She would repeat people's names to make sure that they were who she thought they were. Even when she went back to school she would double check her answers on tests and then double check the professor's corrections to make sure he wasn't giving her credit that she didn't deserve. She did love Richard, in her way, and perhaps now she was going to lose him along with the farm. Everything seemed to be going down hill in her life and even thoughts of 'checking out' were coming back into her mind.

She flopped down on the sofa and then quickly sat up. She was in her riding clothes and she shouldn't be on the good couch.

"What the hell am I thinking?" she asked herself. "It's not a new couch anymore, it's over ten years old. It's mine now, not my parents, and I don't have to answer to them anymore. I can do what I want to do."

And right now she wanted to cry. She buried her face in a throw pillow and wept softly thinking about Richard's statement. It did hurt ...in the mind.

3 THE SEARCH

Sleep didn't come easy that night. Kate woke several times and even tried to contact Kristin, but nothing seem to work -- only her thoughts.

Morning came, as so many had come before. She made coffee, listened to the morning news and thought more about everything. She gave more though about the voice out in the potato field. "You are near. You are near," she said aloud. "What did she mean? Was I near where Kate died or near something else?" Kate realized that she was talking to herself -- aloud. She felt her face get red and then realized that there was no one around to see her talking or being embarrassed. She turned the coffee pot off and went to a corner cupboard. She took out a canteen, rinsed it, and then filled it with water from the tap. From another closet she took out some beef jerky and some dried fruit rolls. She put them in a paper bag and then took the bag and the canteen out the door with her.

Kate walked toward the barn and Shasta greeted her with a low whinny. Kate put the paper bag in her saddle bags after she saddled up and had the bags on the horse. She tossed a coil of rope and her canteen over the saddle horn. She opened one of the steps of the mounting stairs and took out a rifle and a scabbard and put them on the saddle. She then climbed the stairs and got on Shasta's back.

Again, the horse headed in her usual direction, only to be directed toward the old overgrown path. Somehow the ride was not as frightening as it was yesterday. As she rode, Kate's eyes darted back and forth looking for some sign, any sign, of an Indian camp. Soon she saw the concrete bridge at Bika Crossing. She guided Shasta across the drainage ditch, over the downed fence and into the potato field once again. They stopped at the large rock as they had done the day before. From her high perch on Shasta's back she scanned the area. Everything seemed normal and it was a beautiful day.

There were no clouds, no wind, no swirling leaves, just a typical cool, Fall New England morning. She slid off of Shasta onto the big rock and then down to the ground. She looked for, and found, the depression in the earth where she had found the bowl. Kate looked around the depression and kicked at the earth with her boot. In the little run-off ditch where the bowl had rolled she again noticed the dark hole in the earth.

"Shoot," she said, "I should have brought a flashlight."

She knelt down and adjusted her eyes to the dark hole. A slight draft came from the opening. She found another stick and probed into the small dark area. She again felt nothing.

"Shasta," she said, "Come here girl." The white animal stopped eating the grass and moved over to Kate. Kate reached up and got a hold of the coiled rope and unrolled it. She found a rock about the size of coconut and tired the rope around it four or five times so it would not fall out. Kneeling again, she tossed the rock into the darkness.

The rope started to whip into the opening and Kate grabbed it tighter before the entire twenty-five feet disappeared. She felt the snap of the rock stopping at the end of the rope and she then felt the rock swinging back and forth. It wasn't hitting anything.

"That's strange," she thought, "it must be an old cistern or well."

She found another rock and tossed it into the hole. There was no sound. She pulled the rope back up and untied the large rock. She then tossed the rock into the blackness and listened. There was no sound of it hitting bottom.

"Well," she thought, "maybe tomorrow I'll bring a flashlight and see if I can see anything."

Kate pulled herself up by grabbing the saddle and when she was standing she took the canteen off and took a swig of water. She opened the saddle bag and got out her jerky and fruit rolls. She took a bite from a fruit roll and continued to look around the area. Shasta munched on the lush green grasses.

About ten feet away, lower in the drainage ditch, she noticed that the ground was a lot darker than where she was standing.

Shasta was now some 17 to 20 feet away, so she stuck the jerky and fruit rolls in her shirt pocket and put the canteen strap over her shoulder. She carefully moved down the drainage ditch toward the dark earth. As she got closer she realized that the ground was darker because it was wet. Probably a spring or run-off spot made it damp. She turned around to start back up the ditch toward Shasta.

Suddenly, a déjà vu feeling of uncontrollable falling overcame her as she realized that she WAS falling. She was being swallowed up by the earth.

She screamed. This time she could hear herself scream and she could see dark sand-like earth sliding by her. She stopped falling and could feel a sharp pain in her leg and chest.

She didn't know how long she was 'out,' but she knew she had to be. She wasn't sure if she had the wind knocked out of her or if her mind just tried to block out what was happening to her and shut her systems down.

Her leg didn't hurt anymore and then she realized that dirt covered her legs. She remembered dirt and rocks pouring in on top of her. The panic that she was alive and buried, overcame her and she screamed.

Now, everything was quiet. She could hear nothing.

"Help!" she screamed. She heard herself yell. She could see daylight above her -- maybe 15 or 20 feet up. She breathed heavy, trying to regain her composure and control her mind.

Her arms felt good, no hurts.

She struggled with her legs, but they were covered. She was covered with dirt up to her chest. Her eyes adjusted to the darkness and she saw what looked like a large cavern. She could not tell how big it was, but she was in a huge cave. She then realized she was pushing and shoving dirt away from herself as she was looking. The trapped feeling was leaving her mind and she felt she had hope. She was okay, but she knew that she was in a predicament.

Kate dug and dug and dug. It took her about 10 or 12 minutes to free herself from her dirt entrapment. Her legs were fine. She felt that at least there were no broken bones and that the soft earth had probably prevented bones from cracking.

Now, to the problem at hand -- how to get out of here.

She had the rope with her, so it must now be under more dirt. She dug until she found it and pulled it free. She also found her canteen. The strap must have broken in the fall, but at least she had water. She remembered the jerky and fruit rolls -- and food. The piece she had been chewing on was all full of dirt so she spit it aside.

She struggled to her feet which was not an easy chore. She tossed the rope a few times toward the opening above her but all she got was more dirt and rocks to fall on her. She didn't want to call Shasta, because she thought that Shasta's weight might bring the animal down on top of her. She yelled as loud as she could for Shasta to go home.

"Barn, Shasta. Go to the barn girl." She heard nothing and did not know if Shasta had heard her.

The sound on the other end of the phone told Richard that it was ringing in Kate's house but that she was not answering.

"I guess I'll try again, later," he thought, "She must be in the barn feeding Shasta."

He put the phone down and looked out of his office window. He watched as an ambulance quickly backed up to the Emergency Room doors, three floors below. He thought of the day they brought Kate into the hospital some seven years ago. He had just finished his residency and he was now a 'full-fledged' surgeon.

Richard was on-call and quickly got into his greens, ready for anything. The paramedics had alerted them that an old covered bridge had fallen into the Saco River under the weight of two riders and their horses.

More calls told the surgical team that one girl was pronounced dead at the scene and the other was being taken to the hospital. A portion of the girl's skull appeared to be 'mush-like,' indicating possible fractures of the 'frontal, malar, temporal and the zygomatic arches.' Richard was glad that Dr. Williams was still in the hospital and that he had agreed to assist in any surgery.

Kate was not a pretty sight when they wheeled her in. He remembered picking up her eye lid and seeing the white of her eye being blood red. He remembered calling for the on-call ophthalmologist. A cat-scan confirmed the initial thoughts on bone damage and he remembered the eight-hour long surgery that followed. Kate had been his first major patient and he felt real good about how she successfully came out of the operation. He thought about Kate's parents patiently waiting for news about 'the daughter that was not killed.' He never knew or had never seen Kristin, yet he tried to console their parents. They were distraught about Kristin, but were happy that both girls were not taken from them. Kate and Kristin's parents were now only a blur in his memory, but Kate was not.

He recalled her feisty nature and how she fought to control her mind. He remembered how she pleaded with him to remain as her 'personal physician,' long after his duties as her surgeon was no longer required. He also remembered Kate's remarks about him using her as a 'research project' and how much truth there was to her statement.

Richard was fascinated by the young girl that had everything against her and had only her mind to fight off that opposition. She had indeed brought him recognition of his peers when his paper was published by the *New England Journal of Medicine*. He also knew that he had seen her save her professor's life on a rocky ledge on a mountain and how his interest in her was becoming more 'personal.'

He tried Kate's telephone number once again, but there was still no answer. He tried her cellphone number which he had on his speed dial... both on his office phone and his cell phone.

Kate moved around the large subterranean room very cautiously on her hands and knees. She held on to the rope that she had secured to a small stalagmite a few feet away from where she had fallen. She thought how wonderful it would have been if she had found this underground cave when she and Kristin were kids. They would have explored it like they did the small caves down by the river. She thought about the small caves. They weren't far from here. They were made from the swirling water from large winter runoffs. She also remembered the doll she had left in one cave and how, in the spring, the water cleaned out the cave and her doll was gone. She remembered crying because she lost her. She remembered the doll's yellow plastic raincoat. She even remembered the doll's name -- *Margaret*.

Kate tried to determine directions by the placement of the sun, but that was impossible because of the small opening she had fallen through. She could see no point of reference or in what direction the sun was moving. She figured she was in her 'hole' for a least two hours by now.

The path she picked seemed to be obstructed by rocks that tapered to the floor of the damp cavern. Collecting the rope, she followed it back toward the stalagmite and the only source of light. Kate ate a little jerky and took a small sip of water and then tried going in the opposite direction.

This course seemed to take her 'down hill' -- lower and lower in the cave.

There was a light up ahead, coming in from above. She was almost out of rope again and she was approximately under the light. She was crawling on her hands and knees, looking up at the luminous shaft, when her hand didn't hit the ground. She fell forward. She held onto the rope with her other hand, as she was dangling in mid air from her chest up. She inched herself backwards with the help of the rope. She could see a wall about ten feet away, but she knew there was no surface between herself and that wall. The small light above her must have been the hole where she first probed with the stick. This is where she threw the rope in with the rock on the end of it, and this is where she heard no sound when the rocks went in.

She felt around the cave floor and found a stone. Gently she tossed it into the blackness ahead of her. It seamed that a few seconds went by and then she heard a dull 'thud' sound as it hit down below. She felt relieved that she had not crawled into the abyss.

Kate felt better now because she now also knew in what direction she was moving in. The small hole on the surface was west of the hole she had fallen into. The river and road were east of the openings. She thought about it and then got the impression that it really didn't matter, if this chasm was as far as she could get.

Richard put his cell phone down and turned to a nurse that was on duty at the floor station where he had stopped.

"Diane, will you tell Dr. Silverman that I will be leaving shortly. And, I know it's not your job, Diane, but would you call my service and tell them I will be at the Coletrayn number."

"Yes sir, I would be happy to do that for you. And please say hello to Kate for me, will you?"

"Ah, yes ...I will." He tried the same number he had been trying to get for the past four hours. He listened for six or seven rings and then hung the phone up.

"I hope I didn't upset her by what I said yesterday," he thought to himself as he walked into his office. Richard took off his white coat and tried the number again. Nothing.

"She usually tells me where she is going to be," he was thinking, "Maybe I am too protective of her... I don't own her." He laughed as his thought. "No one could ever own Kate Coletrayn."

Kate could now see an opening in the wall across from her and she felt a draft or a gentle breeze coming from it. She found another stone and threw it into the opening. She could hear it ricochet down, what sounded like, a masonry hallway. There was no way to get to the other side, so she started to look in other directions. Crawling, in what she now knew was in a north direction, her hand hit something sharp. She let her eyes focus again and picked up the object. It looked like another brooch or metal item, almost like Kristin's silver brooch, but smaller. She placed it in her shirt pocket and continued the 'feeling' movement forward.

Richard's car moved quickly up the driveway and threw small stones when he made a quick, turning stop by Kate's back porch. He took the porch steps in twos.

Richard banged loudly on the back screen door. He pounded again and then opened the screen door and rapped on the door window.

He tried the door knob. It was unlocked. He opened the door and yelled, "Kate? Kate! Are you here?"

There was no answer. From the kitchen, he looked into the living room. Nothing. He noticed the empty coffee cup in the sink as he headed for the hall to check out the rest of the house.

Now outside, he headed for the barn to see if her horse was gone. At the barn he heard the familiar whinny of Shasta and turned back toward the house when he didn't see Kate. Richard was puzzled. "If she isn't out riding," he thought, "...maybe she's out shopping."

"She left her door unlocked and a cup in the sink ...not like her," he said aloud. Shasta whinnied. He turned and saw Shasta in the barn.

"How come you are not in the corral, girl?" he said as he cautiously moved toward her. He then noticed that she had her bridle and saddle on and he saw the rifle. He ran to different parts of the barn to see if Kate was in there someplace. "Could she have fallen," he asked himself.

She wasn't in the barn. Richard paced back and forth while Shasta looked at him.

"Where is she, girl? Where is Kate?" The horse moved her head up and down and whinnied.

"Com'on girl, be like Lassie and tell me where she is." The horse moved toward the oat barrel. Richard followed her, took her reigns and led her into her box stall. He gave Shasta grain and hay, as he had seen Kate do, after he took the saddle off. He put the rifle and scabbard, out of sight, under the platform part of Kate's mounting stairs.

Richard ran to his car, picked up his cell phone and quickly dialed a number. He put his mechanical horses into gear and drove down the driveway. The local police department answered and he explained the situation to them. The police dispatcher told Richard that they are supposed to wait a certain length of time after someone is reported missing, but, "under the circumstances," she would contact the Search and Rescue Team.

Richard looked along the sides of the road and along parts of the river bank that could be seen from the car, as he headed toward Bika Crossing.

Kate had found an old tree branch that had fallen into, or had been thrown into, the cavern. She reviewed the alternatives she had, and there weren't very many of them. Probably the most sensible thing to do would be to stay put and wait near the opening.

"They will look for me, won't they," she though. She and Richard were supposed to go to the movies and maybe, when he came out, he would look. "But that wouldn't be for six or seven hours ...and how would he know where to look? Maybe Shasta is still up there grazing." She looked at the old tree branch.

"Maybe," she thought, "I could rub some sticks together and start a fire. Not too good," she answered herself, "I couldn't do that, even when I was a Girl Scout."

She thought that the tree limb could reach the hole on the other side of the pit, but she didn't know if it could hold her weight.

"And what if I *do* get across, then what? If I don't fall in, or if the branch doesn't break, what would I do over there?" She thought and then continued talking to herself. "Air is coming from that hole; there might be an other way out of these catacombs."

She sat there reviewing each option that she could think of, as she chewed on a little more fruit role.

Richard had reached Bika Crossing and was backing up to turn around to look again along the road. A Jeep came over the bridge. A revolving, yellow light on the vehicle's roof began to flash. The Jeep pulled up alongside of Richard's car.

"Dr. Sprague?" the driver asked him.

"Yes, Are you from S&R?" he asked the man.

"Yes, I am. I'm Bill Thornton. I own the farm on the other side of the river, and I heard the call on my scanner. What's the story?"

"Kate Coltrane's horse was at her barn, with saddle. I think Kate might have been thrown or she may have fallen."

"Kate is an excellent horsewoman, but she *could* have run into some kind of trouble. Look, Doc, why don't you go back to her house and meet the rest of the S&R unit. The house is going to be the Command

Post. Tell them I'm in the old potato field and I will work my way down toward the river. Jess Hillard is in charge. Okay?"

"Yes, good. I'll go back and tell them. Good luck, Bill."

Richard watched as the Jeep bounced across the drainage ditch.

Kate could hear what sounded like a truck. She thought that it was probably one of John Potter's big rigs hauling chickens to market. Her thoughts then went back to the tree branch that she was bouncing on. She had carefully propped it up against some rocks and was checking her weight on it. No breaking -- so far so good. Next she tied the broken leather strap together and put the canteen over her shoulder. She arched her back and stretched a little. It felt good to stand up and it made her knees feel better also.

Kate made a bowline knot on the rope. She slipped the end onto a short stalagmite and looped the other end under her behind and then tied it around her waist.

Kate struggled to stand the tree branch up. She balanced it on its base while she looped the middle part of the rope around the top of it. With her boot against the base of the branch she carefully lowered the old wood down by feeding her rope through another loop in it. The top of the tree was now into the darkness in the opening across the way. She thought it might pull her into the cavern but felt relieved when it finely touched down on the other side. She freed the rope loops and checked the tied ends again. She rolled and moved the old limb till it seemed steady and secure.

She was ready. She was scared, but ready.

On her hands and knees she slowly started across her newly made bridge. She could feel it flex and bend under her weight. A crazy feeling of "Why didn't I go on a diet?" crossed her mind as a splintering sound filled the underground chamber.

By the time Richard got to Kate's house there were eight or nine vehicles parked in the barn area. Jess Hillard had a topographical map spread out on the hood of a truck. He was pointing out different areas on the map to different men and women. Richard told Hillard that Bill Thornton was already in the potato field, so Hillard called to one of the men and gave him another assignment.

Richard watched as the volunteer group received their orders from their chosen leader. Hillard, a descendant of one of the Pequawkett chiefs, knew the area and he knew the men. His respect had been earned over the years.

Richard thought about the built-in prejudice of Maine. If you weren't born here you were really never considered a 'Mainer.' There was a real dichotomy between native born American Indians, Maine born Frenchmen and Mainers. He wished that Kate was around so he could share his thoughts with her on the subject.

Although Kate was younger than he was, she was wise beyond her years. He thought about the barrier she had built up between them. As far as he was concerned it was all in her mind. Darlene was practically throwing herself on him and Kate was afraid of him. The one he didn't want wanted him, and the one that didn't want him, he wanted.

He knew Kate still had a lot of wounds that were healing, most of them he thought, were self-created. But, in one sense, he was getting tired of waiting for them to heal. As a physician he knew what to do for a wound, but he also knew that time did most of the healing. If only he could find the right prescription to facilitate that healing.

Minutes seemed like hours as Kate edged herself across the frail piece of wood that hovered over an uncertain pit which could, at any second, change, or even end her life.

She heard the truck again. Maybe they were looking for her. All movement on the piece of wood stopped as she debated if she should yell out and risk the movement that might send her down or move on, in the hopes that they would return? The truck noise faded away and she felt the choice had been made for her.

She felt wet and cold and she could feel the perspiration running off her forehead.

She could feel the cold rock of the other side of the opening. She could also feel the drum-like movement of the branch and she realized that it was her heart pounding. For the first time since she had had her skull rebuilt she felt, what seemed like her brain, was pounding against it. Inches to go, but how could she pull herself up from the bent branch? She reached and reached, grasping for anything she could feel to hold on to.

"Pardon me, sir. Are you Doctor Sprague?" Richard turned and jumped back a little as a black round ball of about two inches was stuck into his face. A pimply-faced, greasy-haired man in his early thirties was sticking a microphone at him. The man motioned to his cameraman.

"Channel 26 News, here. I'm Howard C. Bean, 'live' at the farm of Kate Coletrayn. A regional search has been put into motion today, looking for the missing Ms Coletrayn."

Richard turned away and moved out of the video camera range as the man continued.

"Ms Coletrayn is in the middle of a dispute with the State Department of Education's Planning Department over this very land that we are now standing on. As many of you may remember, Kate Coletrayn, along with her sister Kathelina..."

"Kristin!" someone in the crowd shouted at him. "Ah,   Kristin ...were the horse riders that galloped across, and caused the collapse of the old covered bridge that used to span Bika Crossing. Kate's sister

Kathe... ah, Kristin, was killed in that accident. Kate Coletrayn suffered severe brain damage and this is the reason for all the..."

The reporter's last words were never spoken. Richard grabbed the microphone and threw it into the crowd of spectators that has gathered. His hand was up in front of the camera, and he sent it back into the face of the cameraman. He turned to the reporter.

"If you're going to report the news, Bucko, get your goddamn facts straight."

The surprised reporter and cameraman were in shock as Richard headed toward one of the police officers.

Kate's hand touched something that was not a rock or earth. It was almost round, about the size of a baseball, and it has something sticking out from it. Her fingers groped the object in the darkness. It felt like a gourd with a neck on it. Her finger found the neck opening. It bent to her touch. Her fingers continued to feel around until they felt another protrusion. This time it was smaller. She covered it with her hand and then picked up the object. It collapsed in her grip. She released her pressure and it sprang back to its original shape. She dropped it and grabbed for the earth. She was breathing heavy again and took a few deep breaths to regain her composure.

Kate inched her hand along the ground until she felt a large rock. It was something that she could grab.

Slowly, inch by inch, she pulled herself off of the branch and up on to solid ground. She had made it across the 'endless pit.' She sat on the edge of the cavity with her legs dangling into it.

After she felt that her breathing was back to normal she took the rope and started to reel it in. With a few quick snaps, the rope came off of the securing post and fell in the blackness. She pulled the rope up, untied herself and then checked for her canteen and for her few pieces of food. Everything was in order, -- at least her order.

The cool breeze on her wet back gave her a chill. She got to her feet and felt along the wall and floor to make sure there was not another drop-off. She broke the smallest piece of the tree branch off and then, hitting it across her knee, she broke it in two.

"That's funny," she thought to herself, "my leg didn't hurt when I stood on it. I guess I'm too scared to be hurt."

She peeled off some of the dried bark and formed a pile with the bark. She took the two pieces of wood and started rubbing them together very fast.

"I almost didn't get my 'Wilderness badge' because of not being able to start a fire," she said aloud. "Com'on baby now is the time to work," she thought, as she rubbed faster and faster.

Almost, as if the wood understood, it burst into a small flame. She held the flame down to the pieces of bark and, soon, a small fire started to burn. She looked around to see if she could find any more fuel for it. She then saw what she had been touching and trying to identify in the darkness. She screamed!!

There, lying a few feet away from her, was 'Margaret.' The rubber head of her doll was looking up at her. She dropped to her knees and looked more closely at it. It WAS Margaret. She still had the painted eyebrows and the exaggerated red painted lips she had put on her some 20 years ago.

The flame started to flicker and she remembered the task at hand. Kate thought that if she pulled the tree branch she would not have the strength to hold on to it and it would fall into the pit. She looked around, and, as she moved backwards, her head felt something hanging from the top of wall. She turned and saw a wrapped pile of grasses that were tied together in a cone-like shape. A loop-like hole in the rock wall held the grasses.

"It looked like a torch," she thought as she reached for it. Her hands slipped on the bunched grasses. She smelled her hand and the aroma of Cosomoline registered in her mind.

"No, it looks like it could have been an old torch, with grease in it." She pulled it out of the holder and placed it next to the flame. Instantly, light came into the small chamber. Kate held the burning weeds over the pit to see if she could tell how deep it was. She still could not see the bottom. Leaning against the rock wall, her mind reviewed the possibilities of what might have happened if she had not made it across the pit.

Kate placed the torch back into the holder and watched it for a few moments of wonderment.

"Could it be from the Pequawetts?" she said to herself, as she looked around the small tunnel. The old torch settled into a consistent burn as she stooped to permit the light to travel down the tunnel.

The police officers had now ushered off 'all non-essential' personnel from the farm. The television station van sat on the public road at the end of the driveway. Richard turned to the policeman in charge and thanked him for 'tidying up.'

"No problem, Doctor. That Bean guy sticks in my craw. He can twist anything you say into something bad. It's like he is a little dyslexic." Richard chuckled.

"You know don't you that they wouldn't have mounted this big-a search if *you* hadn't been the one to ask for it." Richard gave him a smile as he thought, "If she is out somewhere and hears this on the news, or if she comes home and finds all this going on, she'll hand me my head on a plate."

"My men found a rifle in a scabbard under those steps that go to that little platform in the barn. Does she keep it there?"   " N o , she doesn't. It was on the horse when I found it." The officer, writing in a small notebook, flipped back a page and then said, "Okay, sorry. You did say that there was a rifle on the horse and that the horse was just walking around the barn and corral area."

A police woman, sitting in one of the patrol cars, called to the officer. She held the microphone of the police radio in her hand. The officer walked over to her and took the mike she handed him. Richard decided to check in with his service and started to walk toward his car to use his phone. The police officer called to him.

"Doctor Sprague. *Civil Defense* can't send their helicopter. They have some kind of boat accident off of Old Orchard Beach." Richard shook his head to indicate he understood.

"Cheezum, this is really turning into a 'big deal.' Kate is really going to be 'ticked' at me for starting it," he thought to himself as he started back toward his car again.

Kate had the torch in her hand and stared down the tunnel passageway. Spaced on the walls were other torches, left there as if they were ready to be used at any given time. She stepped over fishing bobbers and parts of fishing poles. She now felt that when the spring run-off inundates the caves by the river, they must flush items from the river into the chamber. Her thoughts give her hope that there was an exit to this strange tomb. She was also excited about the torches and the possibility of this being an Indian camp.

As she made a slight turn in the tunnel, the area in front of her seemed to be get lighter and lighter. Her heart beat faster as she felt that there was the "light at the end of the tunnel -- an exit ahead." Her pace quickened, as it was now easier to see and step over rocks and sticks. The light was becoming brighter and brighter.

Suddenly she was in a big, bright room. But she was not outside.

The room looked as if the ceiling was filled with fluorescent light fixtures. Kate's mind tried to understand what she was seeing. .

It was a large, circular room with Roman-type arches making up the walls.

She walked further into the chamber looking up -- trying to find the light source. The ceiling looked similar to the bowl that she found, almost like crystal pieces. There was a rectangular large stone is in the middle of the room and a series of chair-high rocks around the center rock. She approached the rocks and, when she was a few feet away from them, she stopped dead in her tracks.

There, on the top of the large center rock, was a person -- or what used to be a person. The skeletal remains of a human, partially covered with cloth fragments, was on the rock, facing the ceiling. His or her hands crossed at the skeletal rib cage. She dropped the torch she had been carrying and then quickly moved to the side as the handle part of the torch erupted into flames. Kate's legs felt jelly-like, so she sat on one of the rocks that circled the center rock. The light from the burning pile of what had been the torch was more noticeable than the natural light, as the natural iridescence of the cave seemed to be getting dimmer and dimmer. She rubbed her eyes and thought about the other torches.

She started for the opening she had just come out of and realized she didn't know which one it was -- they all looked alike.

"Doctor. We have checked the entire area and have found nothing. I don't know what to tell you. Tom Harmon is bringing his blood hounds down from Bangor. He should be ready to go in the morning. Ahh, it is getting too dark to search any longer today, but we'll be out again, the first thing in the morning. It's not supposed to be too cold tonight, so if she is out there she should be okay, ...if she's alive."

Richard nodded in acknowledgement and watched as the light on the barn started it's bluish-green ignition that the light sensor has told it to do when it started to get dark.

He thought about the officer's statement, "...if she's alive." He couldn't bare to think that thought -- she had to be alive.

"I'm leaving a man here to keep an eye on the place ...or to let us know if she does turn up."

Richard thanked the officer and then walked over to a policeman that was taking out a sleeping bag from the trunk of his car. Richard handed him a card.

"I'm Richard Sprague," he said, "...my number is here in case you find out anything about her. Please, call me right away."

"I will sir." He said as he took the card. He looked at it and then watched Richard as he walked toward his car.

Sleep didn't come easy that night. Richard woke up several times and called the police department. Everything was the same – "nothing to report."

Kate found a passageway that had a cool draft coming from it and she assumed that it was the one to the 'pit.' It probably was the one, as it had torches on the wall. She took down a torch and held it over the still burning remains of the other torch. It flared into action and she relaxed a little as the light filled the chamber.

The ceiling crystals reflected to other crystals and produced more light than the torch itself could provide. She propped the torch on a rock and ventured a few yards into each of the tunnels and took down any torches that she found. She had accumulated a pile of six or seven of them and placed them a little bit away from the lit torch and the smoldering remains of the first one.

"A fire," she thought to herself as she rubbed her upper arms, "I can gather some of those old twigs and branches and build a fire."

Again, venturing into each of the caves she scooped up branch after branch. She brought them to the central room and she soon had a pile about three feet high. Kate carefully rationed out the amounts that she thought would keep the fire going for the night. She got a small fire going with the help of the second torch.

Everything seemed good -- good as good could be under the circumstances.

Kate had torches for more light when she needed it; wood for the fire to keep her warm; a piece of beef jerky; one fruit roll left to eat; and water in her canteen. She leaned against one of the chair-high rocks and tried to doze. It didn't work so well, because every once in a while she would remember her 'friend' lying on the rock behind her. She would look around to make sure he, or she, was still there, and each time she looked, he, or she, *was* still there. She would try again to sleep.

4 ASHES TO ASHES

Kate didn't think she had slept much that night, but she knew she must have. Most of the wood was gone so she must have added wood several times to her fire.

Light started to fill the chamber once more and she figured it must be morning, because she felt that, somehow, the crystal-like ceiling was reflecting the light from the outside world. She stood up, stretched, and then put the last of her wood on the red coals.

Suddenly, it dawned on her that she didn't hurt. She had stood up, bent down and stood up again... and her leg didn't hurt. She thought about yesterday, the fall, the sharp pain and how she crawled and walked in the tunnel.

She couldn't remember dragging her leg yesterday or any pain at all, as she was all wrapped up with what was happening at the time. She walked around the chamber. She still dragged her foot a little and there was a little pain -- or was it just soreness. There was no real hurting. She was sore and tired, but it did not hurt like it had before yesterday.

She looked at the beautiful colors on the ceiling that were starting to form. Did the ceiling hold some magical powers?

"No, don't be stupid," she said aloud, "...that only happens in Sci-Fi films. This is real and this is now."

Still, there was no feeling of pain. It was almost like it was before her accident. She reached up and felt her head just inside of her hair line. Yes, they were still there. She could feel the 'knots' of 'fishing line' they had used to attach her 'plastic' to her skull. She could feel the knots under her skin so she knew that something had happened with her leg.

Kate thought that she had better look around and try to find a way out of there as she ate a little of her jerky and fruit breakfast. She tried to size up the physical features of where she was. Her analytical mind went into action.

First of all, she had fallen into a pit that was 12 to 15 feet deep. The trench that she called the 'bottomless pit' was 20 or 25 feet east and was 10 or 12 feet lower, or deeper, than where she made her 'entrance.'

The pit. She had no idea how deep it was. There couldn't have been any water at the bottom, because she would have heard the 'splash' of the rocks that she had tossed in. The sounds of the rocks hitting bottom were distant and dull -- perhaps it was sand or soft dirt down there.

The tunnel. The tunnel to the room was across the pit, and after she made it across the opening, the tunnel seemed to move in an upward direction to the room.

The room was 30 or 40 feet across and had tunnel entrances or 'doorways' coming into it -- like the one she use to enter. The tunnels had torches in them but this room had all the light it needed.

She looked up again at the ceiling. When she had searched for wood and torches in the various 'doorways,' she had noticed that they all seemed to go 'downhill.'

"Okay, what does all this tell me," she thought, as she made a wide circle around the room by the arched doorways.

"I found Margaret near the end of the tunnel, and I also found parts of fishing poles and bobbers. Okay, if the water did flush them in here and then the water ran down the tunnels, because of the slope, then water must come into this room also, because that tunnel is west of here."

Kate stacked some reference rocks in front of the opening that she thought she had come though last night. She walked across to an opening that was directly opposite of that tunnel. It had a little larger 'doorway,' so she thought she would try her first 'look-see' of the day.

In the opposite cave she looked at its size but it was too dark to see anything.

Kate plucked a torch from the wall and went back to the remains of her fire in the big room. The torch soon flared up which gave her the light she needed. Kate took her canteen; the little bit of food, her rope, and then she went inside the tunnel.

The cave was a little wider and it sloped *up*, not down. She walked deeper and deeper into the tunnel and wondered if they were natural or man-made.

"They had to be man-made," she thought, "but it must have taken years to cut all of this rock to form them."

She saw what looked like a small gray box up ahead. As she got closer she realized that it was an old car battery, covered by years of salt water washing the outside of it. Kate knew that the Saco River met the ocean about a mile from her house and she knew how the tides sent salt water to mix with fresh water.

Her mind wondered as she looked at the salt-encrusted battery. She thought about cutting holes in the ice of the frozen river and fishing through the hole for smelt when the tides came in and brought the smelt into the river in schools.

"But what about him? ...or her?" she thought, as she turned to make sure 'it' was still there, "...why didn't *it* get washed away?"

Looking closely at the 'body rock,' Kate could make out 'high water marks' about six inches from the top of the rock.

"This room fills with water up to here," she said, as she held her hand a little above her knee, "...and then runs out a tunnel or tunnels. But why the torches? I mean, the Indians didn't look for fishing poles and dolls. Maybe they caught fish and shell fish in here." She started to walk around some more.

"Okay, I have a few ideas of 'why,' but I still have to find out 'how.' Let's see, I traveled about a hundred yards in the tunnel into here. If I was heading east, I would be down by the road or even past it, toward the river."

The battery casing was not damaged and she thought it would have been, being battered by all the water movement to bring it in this far. She tried to nudge the battery with her foot. It didn't move. She pushed a little harder with her foot. Nothing.

She then noticed green colored stranded copper wires attached to the terminal posts on top. Moving her torch so she could see where the wires went, she could see fragments of covering that used to encase the wires. Time and the elements and destroyed most of it. She chuckled to herself.

"Before plastics," she thought. The wires, half covered with dirt and sand, ran along the base of the wall and disappeared in a small hole about 30 feet away. She moved closer toward the little hole and then realized that what she thought was a shadow was a tunnel doorway leading off from the tunnel she was in.

The light reveled that old wooden boards partially covered it. She could see something inside -- but was not sure what it was.

She pushed a board to see if she could see anything more and when she did, the board fell, crashing to the floor. She jumped back a little and saw, what looked like, a rusted door hinge on the board. It *was* an old door. She pulled the remaining boards off of the opening.

Inside the room, up on a two-foot-high, rusted metal frame, were wooden and metal cases. They almost filled the room, from the frame to the ceiling. They were military ammunition boxes.

"Wow," she thought, "An ammunition bunker ...right here in Stillwater Cove. This isn't Indian, and I didn't know the army had anything like this," she said aloud, "...it's, it's..." She held the torch closer and she picked out the words 'Munitionslager Zutritt Verboten.'

"German! This stuff is German!"

Holding the light higher, she estimated that there were 80 to 85 cases of ammunition in there. On a partial stack of wooden boxes, the top one had a broken cover. Kate pulled the broken wood cover off and looked in. There were stones inside, hundreds and hundreds of crystal-like stones. She picked them up and let them fall through her fingers. They were red and green and yellow and... and they looked like tourmaline.

"Was this an old tourmaline mine?" she thought as she forced open the rusted clip that held the lid closed on one of the metal cases. As the lid opened she could smell the odor of Cosmoline. She saw neatly packed rifle ammunition. A small tan paper was on the top of the bullets. It was written in German. "Bei-Aufsichtsleamte W. Kruger. "By Inspector W. Kruger."

"Na," she thought, "...the Germans couldn't have been here and... no, they wouldn't have been mining for tourmaline."

She could not think of any other explanation.

Back in the main tunnel again, she thought she would light one of the wall torches to see better. She looked up and saw a cage-covered light bulb. Two old electric wires ran parallel down from it, turned at white, round, spool-like things and then continued along the wall, at about six feet above the floor. Her eyes followed the wires along the wall to a metal box near another doorway opening.

"What is delaying those dogs," Richard asked Jess Hillard.

"I don't know. He was supposed to be here at six this morning. It's only three hours from Bangor. Bob Whitmore is putting a trace on him. Oh, and the *Coast Guard* said they could send a helicopter over by nine. In the meantime, we are going over every inch again. The Scarborough Unit is also sending over some people to help. We are widening the search."

Hillard wasn't quite sure how to ask his next question.

"Has Kate been known to just disappear like this before?" Hillard paused, then continued before Richard could answer. "..I mean, I heard that she had her skull crushed. Would, ...or could, that have caused any... any damage?"

"*No!* She's never done this and she probably has more brain power than all of your men out there... combined."

Hillard realized that he had touched a very sensitive nerve on the doctor.

"Something is definitely wrong. She has a bad leg and if she fell or something, she might be trapped somewhere or unable to get up," said Richard.

"We're checking it all again, I also have a man checking out the river caves."

"Oh, and if you see the divers will you tell them to call into base."

"The river caves? Where are they," Richard asked.

"There is a series of wash-out caves right where the river bends, just this side of Bika Crossing. The river gets shallower on the other side of the bend. I guess the tide waters only go as far as the bend and the water movement cut holes into the banks ... a few million years ago."

"Weren't they checked yesterday?" Richard asked.

"One of the men took his boat up the river and looked as he went by, but no, not inside."

"I'm going to take a ride over there; I'm going stir-crazy staying here."

"I understand Doctor. I hear she means a lot to you." Richard looked at Hillard. "Ross Norton is going over, why don't you ride with him?"

"Thanks Jess, I will."

"Ross has a radio, so if we hear anything we'll get in touch with you."

"The divers?" Richard asked.

"Yeah, the scuba divers. They are checking the river bottom for a bod..." He stopped in mid-sentence and then continued, "...it's strictly routine, Doctor."

Holding her torch high in the air, Kate looked into the next chamber that went off the main tunnel. It was a carved-out room with a table, chairs and bunk beds near the sides. In the corner there was an old foot locker. Kate carefully opened it. There was a pile of old newspapers and magazines inside. The magazine on top was an old *LIFE* Magazine, dated February 20, 1943.

"Maybe they weren't Germans," she thought, "but where did the German bullets come from?" Kate looked around. She saw another little room.

This room had boots stacked and rubber boats folded neatly on a crude wooden shelf. Next to them were stacks of moth-eaten clothes with German U-boat insignias. It looked like enough gear for several men for several months had been stowed here before the moles and rats ate their share. Cartons and crates lined other shelves and only unidentified tin cans were left in them. The rats even ate the paper labels, if they ever had them to begin with.

Kate picked up a metal encased, photograph. She blew dust off of the glass and looked at a picture of two smiling people with two children on their laps. The man was a German Naval Officer and the woman beside him had on a fortyish style women's jacket.

"Where did these guys go?" she wondered, "Why did they leave in such a hurry that they didn't take things like photographs and the jewels? Were they caught? Were they waiting to link-up with other military personnel?

And who was the man back there," She now was sure that the skeleton on the rock was a man, "...on the rock in the big room." Up until this point she had thought that it was an Indian, but now she wasn't so sure. The scenarios that Kate thought about were mind-boggling. As she continued her exploration, she wondered if she should take any of the items to 'prove' the existence of Germans being here, but decided against it.

"If I *do* get out, I can always lead others back here for any proof."
She thought about what she just said aloud.

"If I do get out, cheezum, I had better get out. I have only seen one 'person,' so the others must have gotten out. And how did they get in? The rafts! They had to have come up the river on those boats, so there has to be an opening."

As Kate progressed further into the tunnel she found more and more side rooms off of the main corridor. Most rooms had crude signs above the doorways - Quatsch.

Each 'Quatsch' held a new 'discovery', but most of them had one thing in common ...a bed. Some of them were army-style cots; others were framed rope hammocks, with most of the ropes eaten away. There were even a few of them that had had mattresses on them, that were now barely recognizable as such. She wondered just how many men had lived in here.

One room had a sign by the doorway - Radiogerat. That room contained all sorts of, what appeared to be, old radio equipment, or what she should it may have looked like. She found several piles of burned papers on the floor.

"On the floor," she thought, "...then water didn't come into this tunnel."

"OH-oh," she said aloud as she peered into a room.

Lying back in a large chair was another skeleton. Its arms hung toward the floor on each side of the chair and a German Lugar was attached to his right hand. His fore finger was still on the trigger. There were parts of a turtle-neck sweater on him and he had on a knit hat. It was easy to see the small round hole in the side of his skull and the gaping hole on the other side. She stooped over and picked up a 9mm shell casting.

"Wow," she thought, murder? ...or suicide? ...fifty years ago. ...wow."

On the other side of the skeleton, a few feet away on the floor, was a small, flat metal case, like an old cigarette case. She picked it up and looked at it. It had engraved letters on it - 'Kapitan Karley.' Kate tried to open it. It was stuck, so she slid it into her shirt pocket. She heard it hit the brooch that was already there. Kate made a quick exit from that room.

She was still thinking about the seated man when she walked into the next room and past a sign that read - Kartenraum. She saw a map on one of the walls. The names were all in German. The drawing had a 'sun-burst' or 'spoke-like' appearance to it.

"Could it be a map of this place," she wondered as she held her torch closer to it to get a better look.

At the hub on the map, she read 'Zentrale' which she believed to be 'center' or 'hub.' On one of the 'spokes' she saw a series of perpendicular 'U' shaped lines coming off of it. The closest one to the center room had a skull and cross-bones and the words 'Munitionslager - Zutritt Verboten' on it.

Her finger followed that spoke down to a spot that had the word 'Drehpunkt' penciled at a place where the width of the spoke seemed to start to get larger and more 'cone' like or 'fan' shaped. Those lines ended at semi-parallel lines that ran down the entire right side of the map and almost formed the letter 'J.' Inside those lines there were, what looked like, nautical markings and the word 'RIVERSACO.'

"Could this be the river and the way out," she asked herself.

If that was the tunnel she was in, she wanted to see if the 'bottomless pit' was also on the map. With her finger, she crossed over the big room moving in the opposite direction. Her finger stopped at another series of parallel line with the words 'Grundloser BodenriR' between them.

"Could be," she thought.

Some of the spokes were not as long as others and she thought perhaps that these could be the 'mine shafts' where all of those stones came form. One other spoke went to the 'Grundloser BodenriR' lines and one went to the larger 'RIVERSACO' lines at the right.

Kate felt that she was in one of the exit or entrance tunnels. She tried to take the map off of the wall, but the portion that she had grabbed only crumbled in her hands. She studied the map on the wall for a few more minutes and then continued on her journey.

"There are 10 or 12 of these small wash-out caves, Doctor." Ross said to Richard. "It shouldn't take more than five minutes a cave to check them out. Getting there will take a little more time than that though, because they are at different heights on the river bank."

Richard had taken one of the flashlights that Ross had given him, but he didn't need it in the first two caves, which only went in 10- to 15-feet into the bank. Carefully crawling over large rocks they headed toward Cave number three.

"Are there rattle snakes in these rocks," Richard asked.

"You're not from Maine, are you Doc." Ross replied.

"No, I'm from Boston, but how did you know that I wasn't?"

"Mainers know that there are no poisonous snakes in Maine, so you have to be an out-of-stater."

"You won't hold that against me, will you Ross?"

"Heck no, I've seen what you have done for people around here. You're one of us."

Richard felt that Ross was trying to give him a compliment. They were now at the entrance to the next cave. "I smell wood smoke," Ross said as they went into it a few feet.

"Yes, I can smell it also. I wonder if Kate lit a fire to signal us or to keep warm."

"This cave is deeper and it becomes smaller as you go in further," Ross told Richard. They were in about 50 feet.

"Well, that's it for this one," Ross said, "...dead end." It looked like the end of the cave was covered with rubble by an old cave-in. "I guess the wind pulls the smoke in from outside ...there is no sign of a fire in here."

"The air is a little hazy," Richard said to cover his disappointment.

"Yeah," Ross answered out of politeness, "...let's try number five."

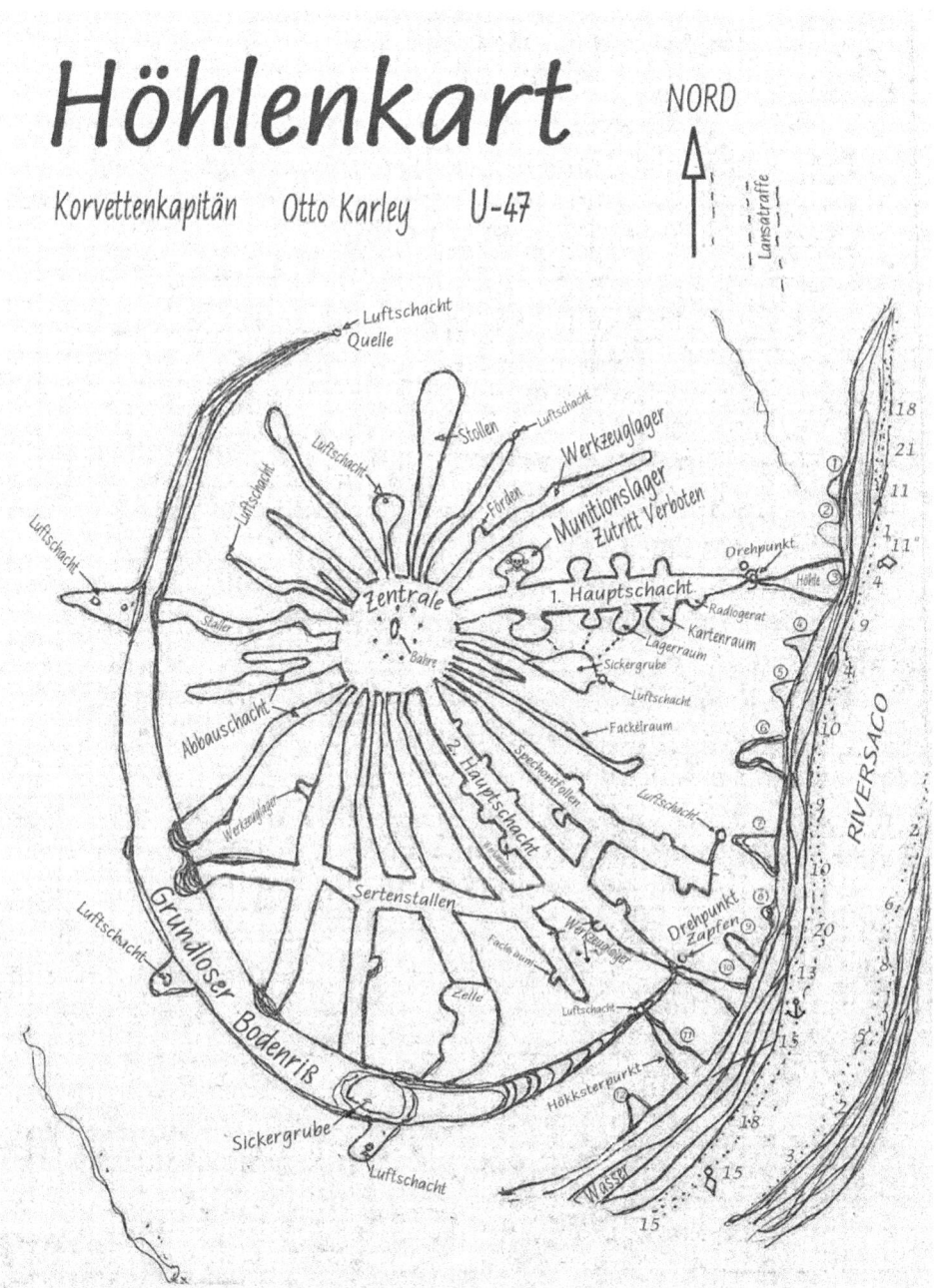

Höhlenkart or Cave Map

Kate listened. She thought she heard voices.

"Hello?" she yelled, "Anyone there?"

No answer.

"H-e-l-l-o-!" she yelled again -- nothing. She thought that perhaps her mind was playing tricks on her, as she rounded a slight bend. She saw what she hoped she wouldn't see - the end of the tunnel. Rocks and dirt piled floor to the ceiling against a big football-shaped rock.

No exit.

She knew that she wasn't crying, but she also knew that there were tears running down her cheeks.　　　"I wonder if the dogs got started yet," Richard said to Ross.

"Let me check." Ross said as he took his radio off of his belt and switched it on. Richard could hear static and, what he thought was, a faint voice. Ross turned the radio off.

"What was that?" Richard asked Ross.

"Static. It will be clearer when we get outside." he said as he switched on the radio once more to show the Doctor. The cave again filled with radio static.

"No!" Richard said as he held his hand at Ross's radio as if to silence it, "I thought I heard someone yell."

Ross turned the radio off and they both listened -- nothing. Ross continued outside to use the radio. Richard tried to listen over Ross's voice as Ross talked to the Command Post.

"Okay, I'm down," Ross said into it and then the radio was silent.

"They're out," he said to Richard, "They let the dogs smell one of her jackets and they took off running toward the barn. They're checking out the barn, real good, right now. He'll let us know if they find anything."

"She is alive, I can feel it ...but she's trapped or caught somehow."

"We'll find her Doc, don't worry."

Worry? That's all Richard could do - worry. Nothing was found in the cave, so Richard wanted to get to the next one quickly. He smelled the odor of wood smoke again as he was leaving.

"When we get a bad winter, I've seen these caves close up with ice chunks. We haven't had any 'real' bad winters for a couple of years now," Ross said,, "They say this year is supposed to be a hum-ding-a. I don't know, I haven't read anything about it in the Farmer's Almanac yet, have you?"

Kate tried to hide her disappointment at not finding a way out, but there was no one there to hide it from.

"Crap!" she said out loud. "Back to square one ...or in this case to 'Zentrale.' She walked back and found the room that had the map in it. She again studied it for two or three minutes.

"Okay, let's see," she said as she counted the tunnels over to the other long one that she thought might come out at the river, "one, two, three, four, five. The fifth tunnel over." Her finger followed the lines on the map as they moved toward the river. Two cross tunnels connected with other tunnels forming a small half-ring around the center room. It stopped at the Grundloser BodenriR lines. She walked briskly toward the center room and once again marveled about how good it was to walk. She still dragged her leg but there was no pain with every step.

She was now in the 'Zentrale' room.

Her eyes had to adjust to the brilliance that the ceiling created. She marked that tunnel by setting up a small pile of rocks at the entrance, and then started to count over five 'doorways.' She marked this tunnel also. A new torch was fired up and the old one was tossed toward the middle of the room. Kate watched it for a few moments as it consumed the handle part.

The inside of this tunnel looked just like the rest of them, torches every fifteen feet or so, and like the other exit tunnel it also went in an uphill direction. A few rooms lined the sides, but they were not as 'finished' as the ones in the other tunnel.

One room, with a sign above it with the word 'Werkzeuglager,' was filled with picks, shovels, shale bars and a few mattocks. With her feet she shoved a few rocks together to mark the doorway in case she had to come back and find a tool. She continued up the slight incline of the tunnel.

By now, Richard and Ross had checked out about four more caves and were climbing toward another. Ross told Richard to wait there a moment while he went down to the water's edge to talk to a boat full of men that were dragging a grappling hook from the back of their boat.

"This can't be the way it ends," he thought as he saw what they were doing; "I don't think I could bear to see Kate come up on the end of a hook ...like a fish."

He turned away and looked at the river bank. Blueberry bushes were arranged is such a way that they looked like they could have been planted along an old path.

The unique bushes ran in a diagonal line down toward the river. Richard became very interested in the arrangement and followed it in both directions with his eyes. They disappeared into the darkness of what Ross had called "cave number eleven."

Ross had returned and gave Richard that there was nothing new to report. He told him that they turned up nothing at the barn and the dogs were now sniffing out the fields.

The two men climbed up the steep grade to cave number eleven.

"Okay, let's see what's in here," Ross said as they switched on their flashlights and went inside. This cave was a lot higher than any of the others and there were many signs that the 'natives' knew about it. Empty beer bottles and cans were all over. There were a few remains of old camp fires, but they were all old and cold. This cave seemed twice as long as any of the others as they continued on. Their flashlight beams went up and down the walls, looking for anything that might tell them that Kate had been there. They reached a point in the cave where they had to bend over to avoid hitting their heads.

"It doesn't look like she has been in here," Ross said. "What do you say we turn around and..." Before he could finish his thought, the ground suddenly started to move under their feet.

"No!" Ross yelled.

"What the..." Richard was saying as his legs started to sink in the soft earth. Rocks and sand and earth came pouring down on them and they were rolling and turning, bouncing and falling and yelling each other's names.

The rumble stopped.

Richard was sweating and he wiped his forehead with is forearm. He called out for Ross.

"Ross? Ross! Are you okay?" There was no answer. Richard could not see a thing, as he franticly tried to dig himself out of his covering. He was almost free when his hand hit something soft. He felt it again and realized that it was Ross. He quickly tried to identify the 'part' that he had touched. It was his face. Richard quickly dug the dirt away from Ross's head and felt his neck for his pulse. He was alive, but his pulse was not that good. Wiggling, and using his knees, Richard managed to get closer to Ross. He wiped his own face and then Ross's. Richard started mouth to mouth resuscitation on Ross. Soon, Ross was breathing on his own and he let out with a faint murmur.

"Ross. Ross, can you hear me?" he yelled when he heard the guttural sound that Ross made. He slapped Ross on the cheek a few times until he heard him say, "What the hell are you doing to me?"

"You're okay! You had me worried there for a moment." Richard tried to brush away more dirt from around him.

"I can't see a thing. Please tell me that you can't see anything either," Ross pleaded.

"Don't worry, I can't either, it's not your eyes. Do you know what happened to your flashlight?"

"Yeah, I still have it in my hand ...under all this dirt."

"Don't let go of it Ross, I'm digging down toward your right hand."

"It can't go anywhere anyway ...it's as stuck as I am. Doc, work on my left hand first, it's up in the air, I mean dirt ...higher than my right hand. If I can free it, I can help you dig."　　Richard　said 'okay' as he started in on Ross's left side.

"Owww," Ross cried, "my legs! They are numb and cold."

Kate cautiously continued along the tunnel she had chosen. She saw a cross tunnel and she stopped. She looked at the map in her mind and thought, "To my left, this cross tunnel dead-ended at one of the other shafts. The one at my right crosses over a couple of shafts and ends at the 'ground looser' - or what ever that is.

She continued to walk straight ahead.

Suddenly, Kate felt a slight gust of wind on her back. As she turned around she heard a distant 'whooshing' sound, then everything got quiet again. She took a few steps back toward the cross tunnel when she heard the faint sound of someone calling. It sounded like someone was yelling 'moss' or 'hoss.' She listened, but that is all she heard. Kate placed her torch in one of the wall hangers and then cupped her hands to her mouth, megaphone style. She yelled as loud as she could.

"HELLO! HeLLo, Can you hear me?"

"Kate! Kate, it's me, Richard. Where are you?" came echoing back. Kate grabbed the torch and moved down the cross tunnel in the direction of Richard's voice.

"I'm in one of the tunnels," she yelled, "...where are you?"

"Tunnels? Ahh, ...I don't know, it's dark in here, our flashlight broke. Ross Norton is with me -- and he's hurt."

"Keep talking," Kate yelled back as she moved down the tunnel, "... how did he get hurt?"

"I'm okay Kate." Ross called out.

"Hi Ross, I'm glad to hear your voice. What happened? How did you get in here?"

"A cave-in. We were looking for you. We were in one of the wash-out caves on the river. The tunnel floor collapsed and we were both buried," Richard yelled, "Are you okay?"

Kate thought about the 'whooshing' noise when he said 'cave-in.'

"I'm fine, keep talking. I'm trying to follow your voice. Are you hurt Richard?" He didn't sound as far away that time, so Kate figured that she was heading in the right direction.

"No, I'm okay. How can you see? Do you have a flashlight?"

"No, I have a torch."

"A torch?" Kate could hear Richard say as if he was talking to Ross.

Kate came to one of the spoke tunnels. She stopped.

"Keep talking," she hollered.

"Where did you get a torch?" Richard called back. Kate could tell that the voice was now coming from the spoke tunnel to her left, and it was getting louder.

She entered the spoke shaft.

"They're all over down here," she answered as she continued; "can you see my light?"

Richard and Ross answered in unison. "No!"

Kate stopped abruptly.

Directly in front of her were bars, steel bars, reminiscent of an Old West Jail. She held up her light to see inside. There, strewn on the floor, were the skeletal remains of three or four humans.

"Kate? Are you still there?"

"Yes," she said quietly, "I ran into a ...an obstacle."

"An obstacle?" Richard inquired.

"Bars," Kate said, as she looked up on the cave wall. She held her torch up to a torch on the wall. The cave soon became much brighter.

"Light! I can see a little light. ...It's coming from about 20 feet away from us and about 30 feet higher than we are," Richard said. Ross concurred, "I see it too."

Kate looked around and then peered deeper into the 'jail.' She couldn't see any bars at the other end, just darkness. She tried to open the jail door, but it would not budge.

"Richard, Ross, I'm going to try to find a way around these bars, are you guys still okay?"

"Yes," Richard yelled back, "Ross is almost free, but his legs are numb and he can't move them. His lower pants legs feel wet, he may have compound fractures."

"Or I could have peed myself," Ross said.

"No, It is blood," said Richard, "I can smell it."

"That's just wonderful," she heard Ross say as she again tried to force the steel door. Kate heard a faint rumble like the sound of distant thunder and then she heard Richard and Ross uttering sounds like, "No, not again,' and Oh no."

"Richard," she screamed, "Richard? Are you okay?"

"Yes. More dirt just fell in on us. I'm moving Ross out of the way of the fall hole. It wasn't as bad as the first cave-in."

"Just be careful, there are big drop-offs in these caves." Kate said, but she then wondered if they were not already in the bottom of the ground looser.

"How does she know about drop-offs," she heard Ross ask Richard. She realized that no one had to yell any more, voices were heard with wonderful clarity. Kate found another wall torch and lit it.

"The light up there just got brighter Ross said to Richard."

"Hang on guys; I'm looking for another way to get to you. I am going to light some more torches to try and give you some light, and then I will be gone for about five minutes. I have to check the map and get some shovels." As Kate backtracked down the shaft, she could hear the guys saying 'map' and 'shovels' and 'what is this place?'

She lit another wall torch and then marked the tunnel she just came out of with stones.

Kate moved very quickly now as she raced down the tunnel toward the big room. She lit about every other torch on the wall as she went by them, leaving behind a trail of light in the caves.

She was in the Zentrale room and the light from the ceiling made it easier for her to find the other exit tunnel. She also lit a few torches in this tunnel as she went by them. Soon she was in the room with the map on the wall.

Her fingers followed the different arms on the map and she figured that she had pin-pointed the spot where Richard and Ross had fallen in. It was at the end of one of the 'Hohle' marks that she now knew were wash-out caves. It was also near one of the small circles on the map with the words 'Luftschlacht' on them. As she looked around the entire map she saw many more 'Luftschlachsts.' She knew that the word 'Luft' was 'air,' so she figured that they were small shafts to bring air into the underground labyrinth.

Back at the map she moved her fingers along the cross tunnel lines to where she thought the guys had fallen in. There was a simple pencil line across the tunnel with the word 'Zelle' next to it. At the other end was a spot where the 'Grundloser BodenriR' got larger and with the word 'Sickergrube' penciled in.

"Okay," she said out loud, "they must be in the Grundloser BodenriR, ground loser, but they must be near the small end of it, and Richard said they were down about thirty feet." Finding her second 'exit' tunnel again, she saw that the Grundloser BodenriR lines ended at a Luftschlacht.

"So, if I get some shovels, we might be able to find the air shaft and dig our way out."

Hope was again charting her ship, she thought as she headed toward the other exit tunnel and the little 'Werkzeuglager' room that contained the digging implements. A lighted corridor was wonderful to see in. She tossed her hand torch to the ground, figuring she would need both hands to carry the three shovels, the pick and the maddox she picked up. She was right!

Kate was back to the cross tunnel she had come out of and also where the wall torches were no longer lit. She put all the tools down except one shovel and took one of the lit torches off the wall. She approximated the length of the remainder of the tunnel she had to travel by the length of the lines on the map. She lit torches as she went and kept watching the ceiling for any signs of an air shaft

As the tunnel narrowed the torches on the wall became fewer and fewer but the shaft was still filled with the red-orange glow of the flames. She now could hear the faint voices of Richard and Ross talking. The voices came from the last small room on the right side of the tunnel.

Her torch filled the room with light and she saw that there were torches on the wall inside. She lit one and looked around. There was a small opening, about the size for one person, on his hands and knees, to crawl into.

"Richard, Ross, can you hear me?" she said into the small opening.

"Yes!" came the simultaneous reply.

"You said five minutes and I don't think you were gone that long," Richard said, "Did you... ah, find shovels?"

"I got them and a pick and a Maddox." Kate said to him through the small tunnel. "Can you see my light," she asked.

"We still see the light, but your voice seems to be coming from the opposite direction."

"Look toward my voice," Kate told him, "do you see any light from that direction?"

"No." they both said.

"Your voice is coming from the direction of where we fell in," Richard called out.

"If my hunch is correct, just on the other side of where you guys fell in, there is a small air shaft that comes up to this level, and then, hopefully, ...outside."

Kate tossed the shovel and her torch up into the small opening and then lifted herself up. There was just enough height to crawl on her hands and knees. She retrieved her shovel and torch. Taking her rope she made a small knot around the end of the old handle so she could drag the shovel behind her as she proceeded ahead. It was difficult holding the torch and using her hand to crawl with.

"We are moving toward the cave-in area," Kate heard Richard say as she crawled along the small cave. As she slowly moved along, eyes darting in every direction, a large river rat ran over her hand and beside her in a hasty retreat to where she had just come from.

"Ahhhhh!!!" she screamed.

"Are you okay? What's the matter?" Richard demanded to know.

"Nothing, I'm fine. I was just making room for a little rodent to run by me." She could here Ross remark about how woman were always so scared by little mice, and he wondered what they would ever do if they saw one of the river rats that lived around here.

As Richard, pulling Ross by his arm-pits, got past the cave-in dirt, he stopped and told Kate where they were.

"We are stopping to rest a moment," Richard called out, "I'm a little tired."

"Are you okay, Richard?"

"He would be if he wasn't dragging me," Ross said.

"Dragging you? You can't walk?" Kate said.

"No, this big galoot is pulling me along the ground ...I owe him one."

"Kate! I see a light up ahead. It must be your torch."

"In what direction is it coming from, and how high up is it," Kate asked.

"It's off to our left and almost at eye level."

"That's good ...just be careful of drop-offs."

"What is this place Kate? How did you get in here?"

I got in here almost the same way you did. I fell through a hole in the middle of the potato field. What it is, is a long story that we will have plenty of time to talk about once we get out of here."

I see your torch!" Richard screamed, almost deafening Ross.

Within seconds, Kate was at the end of the small shaft. She rested on the shaft floor and held the torch into the room where Richard was. Light filled the room.

"Boy am I glad to see you guys."

"Not half as glad as we are to see you," Richard said, "I thought you, and then the two of us, were goners." Ross agreed.

"We're not out of the woods yet," Kate said. She lowered herself into the room. Richard left Ross propped against a rock and was over to her in an instant. They embraced. They kissed.

"Wow," Richard said, "That was some greeting... the best greeting you've ever given me."

"That's because I missed you and I thought I might never see you again. It frightened me."

Richard held her tight.

"That's sweet. I always thought you guys had something going," Ross said.

"Going is the key word," Kate said, "...we had better get 'going' to get you help ...you, you ...voyeur."

They decided that Richard would go into the shaft first and that Kate would then help Richard lift Ross in and Kate would follow. After much struggling and cries of pain, they got Ross into the air chamber. They had fashioned a harness with Kate's rope, and Richard was able to crawl forward on his hands and knees, dragging Ross behind him in the harness. Kate tried to keep the torch high so Richard could see where he was going. Kate told him to feel along with his hands because there was a drop-off into the room at the end of the tunnel. She said that she couldn't see the torch she had lighted before she came into the shaft.

5 THE RETURN

It seemed like it took hours getting into the room at the end of the air shaft. Richard had to turn around in the small tunnel and lower himself into the black room. The torch was passed to Richard who lit another one that was in the room. With light in the room, he carefully lowered the semi-conscious Ross to the cave floor. He then helped Kate into the room.

"He has lost a lot of blood, and his clothes are soaked with it." All three of them looked as if they had been rolling in blood and dirt.

Kate found a piece of wood and Richard made splints using his jacket as bandages. They rested a moment to try and collect their thoughts.

"Okay, how do we get out of here?" Richard asked.

"I'm not sure, but according to the map there are air..." Richard interrupted.

"What is this map you keep talking about? What is this place? Tell me that it's an old Indian tunnel."

"Wrong. Would you believe German? Would you believe U-Boat sailors mining for tourmaline?"

"What? Have you been smelling the fumes from these torches? What are you talking about?" Kate grabbed Richard by his arm to silence him. In the distance the low sounds of hound dogs could be heard barking.

"The dogs!" Richard said, "The dogs are looking for you. They must be near one of the vents." The two tried to listen to see in what direction the noise was coming from. They could not tell. Ross was sleeping as they got to their feet.

"He'll be okay for a little while, but we do have to get help for him... what do we do Captain?"

"Richard, you go up that way as far as the big room. See if you can spot any holes or small openings in the walls or ceiling on the way and mark them with rocks. I will look around the end of this tunnel and then try the cross tunnel."

"The big room? ...Cross tunnel? Kate, what is this place?" She was out the door but he heard her say as she left, "I told you, but all you did was make fun of me."

Richard went in the direction that Kate had told him to go, thinking about her statement.

Kate got a fresh torch and carefully looked all over the end of the shaft. Nothing that she could see gave her any idea of how to get out. She went back to the room that Ross was in, checked on him and then headed toward the cross tunnel.

She thought that this tunnel was the one that came to a dead-end into one of the spoke tunnels. She turned in the direction that she knew was the river and, if she remembered the map correctly, to another air shaft.

Richard's mouth opened in amazement when he entered the big, light-filled room. He stared at the ceiling as he walked deeper into the room. He was a little shook up when he put his hand on the Tibia and then felt the Fibula of the man lying on the rock table. He moved quickly to the entrance of the tunnel he had just emerged from. The torches gave him plenty of light and he looked all around, because he really wasn't up for any more sudden surprises -- like the guy back there.

Kate had exhausted all rooms, nooks and crannies. She went back to the room that Ross was in. He was quietly resting in the corner. She sat on a chair-like rock and tried to be calm and collected, but she knew it wasn't going to work. She could feel the empty feeling and her emotions were building up in her throat almost like she was going to be sick.

"Hear we go round the mulberry bush, the mulberry bush, the mulberry bush." She heard someone singing. She stood up and looked around.

"Kristin? Are you here?" There was only silence and a few yelps from dogs away off in the distance somewhere.

"Kristin, you told me I was 'near' and then I fell in here. Are you telling me how to get out?"

"Oh good, he's awake." Richard said as he walked in the room. Kate spun around in surprise. . "Was he talking to you, Kate?" Kate ran to him and held on to him. "Are you okay? What's the matter?" Kate was crying. "Is it Ross?" he asked, "...he didn't di...ah, Kate? Kate, talk to me!"

"She sang to me Richard, Kristin sang to me."

"What? Kate, I know this has been a strain on you but ...singing?"

"She did Richard, she sang 'Hear we go round the mulberry bush,' ...honest." He held her tightly.

"Richard, she gave me the message about how to find this place. I think this was a message on how to get out."

"What? She talked to you about these caves? When? How?"

"Richard, sing me the words to mulberry bush."

"What?"

"Sing, it has to be a clue."

Richard felt kind of foolish singing the song, and then while he was singing it, Ross woke up and heard him singing and went back to sleep.

"Richard, what do kids do when they are singing it? Someone holds up their hand and the person in the middle circles, or pivots, on that person's hand. That has to be it, she is telling us about a pivot."

Richard didn't ask any more questions, he just followed Kate out into the tunnel corridor. Kate went immediately to a huge, football shaped rock, which went from floor to ceiling in the cave. She pushed on the one side of it.

"Com'on Richard, push!" she said. Richard pushed with her. Suddenly the rock started to move. The rock started to turn. Soon, it was at a ninety degree angle to where it was when they started. Cool air rushed in as if to greet them.

"We did it Richard, this is the way out. I'll go up ahead and see where it comes out. See if Ross is well enough to move or if we should get someone in here with a stretcher.

Richard just shook his head in amazement as he watched her pick up a torch and disappear into the tunnel on the other side of the pivoting rock.

As Kate quickly walked through the tunnel she heard her name.

"Kate."

It's Kristin, she thought. "Kristin!" she said, "...thanks."

"You are near..." the voice said and then faded away.

"You are near..., that's what you said in the field." Kate looked around her and as she did she tripped and fell, twisting her ankle. She sat there for a few moments and rubbed her ankle and, as she did, she saw a hole in the side of the cave. She retrieved her torch before it burned the handle. She looked into the hole. There were silver brooches like the one that she had found in the caves below and there were bowls, silver arm bracelets and spear and arrow heads - most made of tourmaline. "The Indians were here, and Kate was telling me that."

"The ambulance went screaming away. Your dad and I watched it disappear into the twilight of that afternoon. Ross was in it and he was doing fine. I gave a rough map of the caves to Jess Hillard, and a Policeman was posted at the wash-out cave entrance that I had come out of. We learned that one of the hounds had fallen into the hole that I had fallen into. It took them four hours to lower a man into the hole and get the dog out. They were about to send a search party into the hole for me, when they got word that Richard and Ross were lost. They stopped the group from going into the hole and concentrated their efforts at the river where Richard and Ross had last been seen. Everyone was shocked when I walked up to them and told them that they needed an ambulance for Ross."

"You just walked up to them and told them that?" Karley asked.

"Yes, what was I supposed to do, jump up and down and say I'm alive, I'm alive!"

"M-*om*-m-m. I meant, is that how it all ended?"

"Not all, sweetheart, they opened that little case that I had found and, through an interpreter, they discovered that it was the journal of the German Captain."

"What was in it? huh? huh?"

"Easy, Karley. It told how they were in a German U-Boat, number U-47 or something like that, and they had been patrolling up and down the Maine coast. Apparently they had done it for two or three years. They realized that their submarine had a slow leak, after it had been dashed against some rocks near Biddeford. They found out that they couldn't get home.

They had apparently discovered the wash-out caves some time before this had happened, so, by night, they sent rubber boats in with all kinds of gear. They discovered the 'Hohle' or subterranean caves and realized that this was an old Indian manufacturing spot for making spear heads, arrow heads and bowls out of the tourmaline.

By the time their boat finely sank, they had removed all the provisions and movable contents from it into the caves. And, they had established their 'Hauptquartier,' or headquarters in the tunnels."

"But how come no one ever saw them and where did they get all their food?"

"Well, they did have some food on board, which they brought in and, eventually over the year and a half that they were there, they went into Stillwater Cove, Saco, Biddeford, and Old Orchard Beach. They had civilian clothes and they acted like American citizens. The journal told about one of the men, who had no accent, did all the talking when they went shopping. It even said how the man would talk with other shoppers and that one woman had even invited him to her house for a home-cooked meal. She thought that he worked in the boot factory."

"Wow, right here in Stillwater Cove. What about the jail and all the dead guys?" Karley inquired.

"In the winter of 1943-44, I guess the river plugged up all of the caves with ice, and they were trapped inside. It was okay for a while, but when they couldn't find any way out, the men started to get restless. They were well disciplined, but they stated to have small outbreaks of... mutiny I guess you would call it that. The Captain had the jail built and any one that disobeyed him was put into it. Without food and heat, most of them died in the stockade.

"What about the guy with the bullet in him? The guy with the flat case?"

"That was the Captain. He was the last to go and he wrote that he wanted it to end quick, not through starvation. He shot himself."

"What? The last to go? What about the guy on the rock in the big room?"

"Well, they checked his bones and facial structure. His bones were much older and they believe that he was the Indian that was 'swallowed up by the earth.' A note in Captain Karley's journal..."

"Captain Karley! You said I was named after a Sea Captain, but I didn't know that he was German."

"Well, honey, if it wasn't for Captain Karley and his men, and his map, we probably would never have made it out of there... and, if we hadn't, then you wouldn't be here today." Karley said 'wow,' as she sat back to hear the rest of the story.

"Anyway, Captain Karley's journal said that his men had found the 'Indianer' and they built a 'Schrein' or a memorial for him ...and placed his skeleton on the Bahre Rock."

"Captain Karley, wow! And that's when you and daddy started to go out... Wow!"

"That night, they wanted us to go in an ambulance, but we wanted to walk back to the house ...to stretch out legs. Your father told them that we would go into the hospital, from the house, and to wait there for us. Being a doctor, they agreed.

As we walked back, he kept asking me over and over about my fall and the pain. I may still have the limp but it no longer hurts.

'You're the doctor, you tell me,' I would say to him, - over and over. He told me he was worried sick about me and I told him that I missed him too. I told him that I thought Kristin was trying to tell me something and that I wasn't sure just exactly what it was, but if we spent the next sixty or seventy years, we could try and find out, ...together."

"Aw, mom. I love you and daddy."

The Journal was closed.

Author's Notes:
In my last book I told you about dreaming.

I said: "Always do your best, but never forget to center on your dreams."

Writing had been a dream since I was very young. It became a reality for me as a Journalist in the US Navy, but teaching eclipsed that as the main direction after I graduated from **Kutztown State College** in Pennsylvania.

The next shift in focus was a move to school administration, facilitated by studies at **New York University** and then the **University of Maine**.

After an unsuccessful first attempt, I found a soulmate with similar values and ideals.

The focus then shifted to a boy and a girl, creating the perfect sized family.

Family dreams of California became a reality after a time as a museum curator at the **Portland Maine Museum of Art**.

In California the focus shifted to include architectural work on the **Simon Rodia Towers**; the **Will Rogers Home** in Santa Monica; and working in the movie industry in Burbank and Los Angeles.

But Los Angeles was no place to rear children. The objective changed to Northern California; to design houses; teach theatre arts at the local college; help start a community theatre; watch my wife teach Special Needs Children; and finally back to writing.

Newspaper photography and writing brought those unforgotten dreams back to the forefront despite a quarter of my skull being replaced with plastic from a horse accident -- a vivid reminder not to lose that focus on those dreams.

This book looks at many of the mind problems that plagued me while recourporating from my crushed skull. I now have more empathy for head injuries having lived through it.

Back to dreaming.

Our daughter is now married and we have three wonderful grandchildren. One grandson is an electrical linesman in Texas. His brother is a junior in high school and our girl is a freshman.

Son-in-law Jason, a native American, is in construction and writes, directs and produces a television outdoor/hunting show, *Impact Insanity,* with our daughter and several friends.

Our son works in healthcare technology development for **Philips Healthcare** and writes, acts, directs, and produces theatre in San Francisco.

November 2015 marked 46 years of marriage.

I am still focusing on the dream of writing the "Great American Novel" while my wife and I enjoy, or try to enjoy, retirement.

And one of these days, I may actually figure out what I want to focus on in life -- beside dreaming.   -- ***Paul H. Robeson***